THE DAYSTAR VOYAGES

DARK SPELL OVER MORLANDRIA

GILBERT MORRIS
AND DAN MEEKS

jF
Mor

MOODY PRESS
CHICAGO

ISBN: 0-8024-4108-4

1 3 5 7 9 10 8 6 4 2

Printed in the United States of America

This book is dedicated to our children: Mike, Gina, Chris, and April Meeks. You are God's blessing to your mother and me. We can't imagine what our lives would have been without you.

Remember, as long as you have Jesus, you have everything.

We love you!

Characters

Contents

1

Secret Orders

The star cruiser *Daystar* moved silently and with incredible speed through the blackness of space. Mei-Lani Lao sat in her cabin and stared down at what she had just written. At thirteen she was the youngest of the *Daystar* Space Rangers, who formed part of the ship's crew. A petite girl with jet black hair and luminous brown eyes, she was also the smallest, at five one and ninety-five pounds.

Shifting herself to a more comfortable position, Mei-Lani lifted her eyes briefly and looked out the porthole at the millions of stars that adorned the blackness of space. Pursing her lips in frustration, she was looking back down to write when, suddenly, the door to her cabin burst open.

"Hey, Mei-Lani, I want you to—"

Mei-Lani leaped up from her desk and hurriedly concealed her small notebook under a stack of papers. "What are you doing breaking into my cabin like this, Ringo? Get out of here!"

Ringo Smith stopped as abruptly as if he had run into a wall. He stood there obviously confused.

Mei-Lani knew she had the reputation of being the mildest and most gentle-tempered of anyone aboard the *Daystar*. She suspected, however, that right now her face was flushed and her almond-shaped eyes were flashing with anger.

"I'm—I'm sorry, Mei-Lani," Ringo stammered. He was only one year older than she was. Not a large young man, he had brown hair, rather unusual hazel eyes, and was somewhat bashful. "I didn't mean to interrupt. I just was so excited . . ."

"Just get out of here and leave me alone, and don't ever come into my cabin again without asking permission! Do you hear?"

"Why—sure, Mei-Lani. I said I'm sorry."

So confused that he almost forgot why he had wanted to see Mei-Lani in the first place, Ringo closed her door and headed down the corridor toward the communications center. His emotions were churning, and his thoughts centered on one person—not Mei-Lani but Raina St. Clair. Ringo had a crush on Raina—as it was called back in the old days.

When he reached communications, Ringo looked around for Raina and, seeing her, headed toward her station.

Raina was fourteen and very attractive. She had auburn hair, an oval face, and a dimple in her chin. She was wearing the standard uniform for women on board the star cruiser—slate gray tunic with silver trim on the collar and above the cuffs. Her ensign insignia was affixed to her right sleeve, and the *Daystar* Space Ranger insignia was positioned on the left sleeve. Her navy blue pants with a silver stripe down each side fitted her figure nicely.

Ringo thought that she was beautiful—from the top of her head down to her black rubber-soled half-boots.

"Hey, Raina, I need to talk to you."

"What is it, Ringo?" she said, not taking her eyes off the board in front of her. "I'm a little bit busy right now."

"But this is important."

With a sigh Raina turned to face him and smiled briefly.

He supposed she could see that he was troubled.

"What's wrong, Ringo?"

"Well, it's Mei-Lani. I just saw her, and she nearly bit my head off."

"That doesn't sound like Mei-Lani."

"It's *not* like her!" Ringo said quickly. "Never saw her so mad in all my life. Her face was red, and her eyes were flashing."

"What did you *do?*"

"Well, I—" Ringo stopped, and suddenly he felt his face grow warm. "I was anxious to see her about something, so I busted into her cabin without knocking. I didn't think."

"That was very impolite, and you shouldn't have done it."

"Sure. I know. But here's what happened. She had something in her hands. I couldn't see what it was, but she made a big thing out of hiding it, and she had a guilty look on her face."

"You're the one that should have the guilty look, bursting into a girl's cabin!"

Ringo's flush increased. "I know that, but well—well, I've had some guilty secrets myself." He tried to grin and shrugged his shoulders. "I know what it feels like to get caught, and that's what happened. She was trying to hide something that she didn't want anybody to see, and then she blew up just like a volcano, and that's not like Mei-Lani."

"Oh, it was just something personal, Ringo. Maybe a poem or something. Mei-Lani would never do anything wrong."

Then several lights on the board flashed. Raina turned and punched buttons and threw a switch. When

11

she turned back to Ringo, she said, "Mei-Lani's a devout Christian. She and I are prayer partners. I think you misread the situation."

"Maybe."

Ringo shuffled his feet in embarrassment. He had a deep inferiority complex, partly because he had been raised in a state orphanage. He fingered the cord around his neck. It held a medallion that was hidden beneath his uniform. It was always there. The medallion had a hawk or a falcon on one side and the profile of a strong-looking man on the other. There were words on the medallion, also, and what looked like a motto of some sort, although no one could read the language it was written in.

Whenever Ringo was nervous, he fingered the medallion, and now he pulled out the metal disk and rubbed it between his fingers.

"I guess I'll have to tell her I'm sorry. Right?"

"Right." Raina put a hand on his arm and smiled up at him. "Just be careful. Mei-Lani's at a rather dangerous period of life."

"Dangerous? What does that mean?"

"I mean she's not a girl and not a woman. That's a hard time, so just be especially careful what you say, because she's rather sensitive."

Ringo stared at Raina, then asked, "What about you?"

"Oh, I'm a little older. I went through all that last year. Most of it anyway." Raina smiled again, and then her eyes laughed up at him. "And I expect you're going through the same thing. It's just part of growing up, and growing up is hard."

"Sure is," Ringo said fervently. Then he asked, hope in his voice, "Could we have a game of chess when you're off duty?"

"Sure. That'll be fine."

When Ringo nodded happily, then left, Raina went back to work. But she could not forget what he had told her about Mei-Lani. Finally she went down the corridor and stuck her head into a small room where a redheaded boy sat at a table. He was overweight and wore an awful orange and purple bandana around his neck.

"Heck," she said, "would you watch my board for me? I've got an errand."

Hector Jordan turned his blue eyes on Raina and grinned. Getting up from the electronic device he was probing, he came to the door, put an arm around her and gave her a squeeze. Heck was fifteen. "Why, sure, Raina. And, hey, how about you and I get together after work?" He winked. "I mean, after all, the two best-looking people on the ship ought to stay together."

Freeing herself from Heck's grasp, Raina forced a smile and said, "You better ask Jerusha. I'm going to play chess with Ringo."

"*Ringo?* You mean you're turning me down for that nerd?"

"Watch the board, will you, Heck?" Raina said.

She was as accustomed to Heck's enormous ego as she had grown accustomed to his strange clothes. Heck was an electronics genius but, of all the Rangers, could be described as a sneaky individual. He was so selfish, Raina thought, always thinking of his own comfort, and he definitely was not a Christian.

As Raina continued down the corridor, she greeted several of the crew members, including Ivan Petroski, the chief engineer, and Zeno Thrax, the first officer. Then she came to Mei-Lani Lao's door.

"Mei-Lani, it's Raina."

The door opened at once, and Raina stepped inside. "Hi," she said. "I thought we might have time to take a break."

"Oh, I don't really want to go anywhere right now —especially not to the lounge area!"

Raina St. Clair saw at once that Mei-Lani was disturbed about something. The girl was twisting her hands nervously as she sat cross-legged on the couch, and there was an expression in her eyes that was unusual.

"Then why don't you and Dai Bando and I get together with Ringo and have a little chess tournament after we're all off duty?"

"I don't really want to. You three go ahead."

Raina sat down on the couch and put her arm around the girl. "What's wrong, Mei-Lani?" she asked quietly. "You're upset about something."

"Oh, it's nothing important."

Mei-Lani for one moment seemed about to say more, and Raina waited, hoping that the younger girl would tell her the problem.

But Mei-Lani simply shook her head and tried to smile. "Don't worry about me." Then she abruptly changed the subject, saying, "I still haven't got over how Dai saved the situation on the red planet."

"It's a good thing he was there," Raina agreed. "I don't think we could have made it without him." Their friend Dai Bando had been instrumental in discovering the secret of a planet inhabited only by children.

Raina always spoke of Dai with affection. He was sixteen, the oldest member of the Space Rangers. He was tall and had a dark, Welsh handsomeness about him. Perhaps she had more than ordinary admiration for him.

Then she said, "You're sure there's nothing wrong,

Mei-Lani? I know how it is. I get down in the dumps myself sometimes."

Once again Mei-Lani started to speak but then changed her mind.

Raina said, "All right. I'll—"

She never finished her sentence, for over the speaker system came a message indicating that a top-secret communication was coming from Earth.

Like a scalded cat, Raina whirled and scrambled out of Mei-Lani's cabin. Running down the corridor, she bumped into Studs Cagney, the crew chief. She bounced off him, for Cagney was a short, solid, muscular man.

"Why can't you watch where you're going?" he growled. "I always said we'd get nowhere trying to man a ship with babies out of the nursery!"

"Sorry, Chief!" Raina gasped, then stepped around him and sped lightly back to her station.

"Hey, sweetheart, you're about to miss—"

Without apology, Raina shoved Heck out of the way, and her hands began flying over the controls as she intercepted the message.

"I could have handled that!" Heck boasted. "I'm not only the greatest electronics genius in the world, I'm also the best at communications."

Ignoring him, Raina filtered out all other signals and then said quickly, "Captain Edge—a confidential message from Commandant Winona Lee . . ."

Captain Mark Edge came off his cot like a cat. He looked like a Viking, for at six one he was large and strong. He had ash-blond hair and light blue gray eyes that could pierce one like a laser beam. Something in his face was almost hard and revealed his background —he'd been close to being a pirate before being com-

15

missioned by Commandant Lee to command the *Daystar*.

Now he touched a button on his desk and said brusquely, "Route the message to my quarters, St. Clair!"

Almost at once Commandant Lee's voice broke the silence of his cabin. "Captain Edge, are you there?"

Edge sat at the console and flicked a switch so that his image was sent to her. Then he studied her likeness on the screen in front of him.

Commandant Lee was a small, older woman with silver hair and gray eyes. As commandant of the Intergalactic Council, she wielded tremendous power in the system.

"Good to speak with you again, Captain Edge." Her voice was crisp but friendly.

"Thank you, Commandant." Edge nodded. "I would guess you've got orders."

"Yes. Are you certain this message is not being read by anyone else on the ship?"

"Yes, it's on Encryption Code X3. It's operative only on this single communication terminal in my quarters. You may speak freely."

"Very well. Here are your orders, and they're very serious. Are you familiar with the planet Morlandria?"

"Vaguely, although I've never been there."

"Well, you're going there now, Captain Edge. I want you to take the *Daystar* to that planet on a critical mission. Denethor, the king of Morlandria, is going to be assassinated. Your mission is to proceed to Morlandria, investigate, and stop the assassin."

For a moment Edge sat in silence. Then he asked, "Can you tell me anything about the politics of all of this?"

"At this time? Yes. It's a very touchy situation,"

Commandant Lee said, and her lips drew into a white line. "Tell the *crew* nothing."

"It's sometimes a little hard when a crew doesn't know where they're going."

"I'm sorry for that, but in this case we have no alternative," she said. "Just tell them, if you will, that they're going to Morlandria for rest and relaxation."

"But I don't think that's quite fair to either the Rangers or the crew!" he protested. "If there's going to be danger, they have a right to know about it."

But Commandant Lee was firm. "Not this time, Captain! Rest and relaxation as far as the crew is concerned. It may prove to be a very simple undertaking, and all of them may not need to be involved. Let's hope so."

"Yes, Commandant. I understand."

"Keep in touch. I want to know everything that happens." She smiled then.

Edge was reminded of a kindly grandmother, and he knew *that* was a mistake. Though Commandant Lee was kindly, she had a razor-sharp mind and apparently knew everything that was happening all over the galaxy.

"Any other orders?"

"You keep yourself straight on this one, Mark."

The unexpected personal remark caught him off guard. "I always try to do that." He tried to think why she would give him this specific message. Then suddenly it came to him. "You're not worried about me romancing our surgeon, are you?"

"Yes, I am. Dr. Temple Cole is a very attractive woman, and I want nothing to interfere with the mission. You keep yourself fully professional with the good doctor."

"Are those orders?"

"No, I'm making it as a personal request. This is important, Mark. And do be careful. This mission could be dangerous."

"Aye, aye," he said. "I'll do my best."

After the two had signed off, Mark Edge leaned back. "Stop an assassin. Don't tell anyone the real reason where we're going or why. And keep my mind off Temple Cole." He smiled briefly then, and amusement touched his blue gray eyes. "I can do the first two, but I'm not sure about that last."

2

Fun in the Sun

Captain Mark Edge loved to do delicate electronics work. As he squinted his eyes and poked out his tongue unthinkingly, his big hands guided the tiny instrument needed to adjust the Commstat he was working on.

The Commstat was the powerful sender device used for tracking by Intergalactic rangers. Edge had confiscated it from Studs Cagney on their mission to Makon, where Studs had unwisely used it to communicate with one of Sir Richard Irons's shadow ships.

It was a black rectangular box, 1" x 1" x 2" in size, with an activation button on its front surface. Unfortunately, in an angry moment Edge had thrown the device against a bulkhead and broken it. The technology inside the small mechanism was beyond anything he had seen before. He only hoped he was making the correct repairs.

For two hours he had worked, and now he had arrived at the climax. "Just one more little touch here," he whispered, holding his hands absolutely steady, "and we'll have—"

Something cold and wet suddenly touched the back of Edge's neck. He yelled, "Yow!" and the probe he was using stabbed into the Commstat. Sparks shot out, and a screaming whine filled the room as the device blew up.

Whirling, Edge glared at the huge, black German shepherd that now stood wagging her tail and barking happily. He threw down the probe, a flood of anger and frustration filling him. Then he lifted his eyes to the girl who hurried up beside the dog. "I *told* you to keep that dog away from me, Ensign Ericson!"

"I'm sorry, Captain. She got away from me."

Jerusha Ericson's eyes were wide and troubled. Contessa, her super German shepherd, was enamored of Capt. Mark Edge. The extremely intelligent canine simply could not keep from going to him every time he came in sight. And Captain Edge despised all dogs.

Ensign Ericson reached down and grabbed Contessa by the scruff. "I'll take her out right away."

"You'd better! Otherwise I'll shove her out a space port! Look at what happened!" Edge clenched his teeth and gave a despairing wave of his hand toward the destroyed Commstat. "I've worked on that thing for months, and that stupid dog destroys it in one second!"

"I'll put it back together for you, Captain."

"Impossible."

He had to admit that the teenage ensign looked rather attractive as she stood before him. She had blonde hair and very dark blue eyes set in a squarish face. She was strong and athletic, but beyond that she was one of the finest young engineering geniuses Edge had ever seen. And it had been Jerusha who had recruited the Space Rangers at Edge's request when he had been desperate to find a crew. Her Space Academy friends Ringo Smith, Heck Jordan, Raina St. Clair, and Mei-Lani Lao had formed the nucleus of his team for the first voyage of the *Daystar*.

"That dog is *not* going on another mission!" Edge declared. He continued to dress down the ensign for the next five minutes, telling her what he thought of dogs in general and Contessa in particular. But eventually he ran down. "Now, get out of here and don't let me see that beast again!"

Jerusha's lips trembled. "I'm—I'm sorry, Captain."

Edge sighed. He saw tears forming in the ensign's eyes. It was obvious that this tough young lady had a special feeling for him. He cut his dismissal speech short and cleared his throat. "Well, now. There's no need to get all teary about it." He wanted to put an arm around the child to comfort her, but he knew that would not do. Jerusha was *not* a child. At fifteen, she was on the brink of young womanhood.

Can't have anything like that going on, Edge thought. *She's a beautiful young lady, and I've got to keep order on the ship.* Hastily he said, "There, there, now. It's all right. Just take that dog out of here, and I'll try to see what I can do with this mess that's been made."

"Yes, Captain."

Edge watched her go, then turned to look at the Commstat. He shook his head in despair and muttered, "Well, I guess it doesn't eternally matter."

He left the shattered Commstat on the table and headed for the bridge.

As always when he stepped onto the bridge of the *Daystar,* Mark Edge felt pleasure, for it was all a bridge should be. His command chair was located in the exact center of the oval room. He could control every system aboard the cruiser from this location. A giant view screen was directly in front of him with smaller viewers on either side. He could communicate with all his senior staff at the same time. The old *Daystar* had been boxy and uncomfortable, but this new *Daystar,* the 831-B, seemed molded around him like a well-fitted glove.

Walking over to his first officer, he said, "Thrax, did you set the course for Morlandria?"

Zeno Thrax gave Captain Edge a reproachful look. "Of course, sir. You ordered it, didn't you?"

Thrax was rather chilling to look at. He was a perfect albino. He had colorless eyes, and skin as white as flesh could possibly be. But he was a fine first officer.

"I understand it's a fine climate on Morlandria, Captain. Lush vegetation, beautiful oceans and beaches. Not like my home."

Zeno came from the planet Mentor Seven, which consisted of nothing but mines deep under the surface. He had lived most of his life underground with his people, all of whom were albinos.

"I don't see how any of you can stand living in underground caves like moles all the time."

"It's all my people know, Captain." Suddenly Thrax's pale eyes looked sad. "I'd like to go back there someday, but I can't."

Mark Edge knew that, but no one knew why. "Why not?"

Thrax suddenly looked embarrassed, which was a strange thing for him. "It's too long a story to go into, Captain, and I'm afraid not a happy one."

Edge looked at his first officer questioningly but then decided to not go into Zeno's history. On his part, he wished he could reveal their current mission to his first officer, but Commandant Lee had been strict. So he said only, "Call all the crew into the conference room, First."

"Yes sir."

Fifteen minutes later, all of the Rangers and those of the crew that could be spared had gathered.

The conference area was a simple room having large portholes on one side, which gave a good view of the galaxy. The table could accommodate a dozen people, and the Rangers were joined around it by Lt. Tara

Jaleel, the weapons officer; Dr. Temple Cole, the flight surgeon; Bronwen Llewellen, the capable navigator; and Zeno Thrax.

Edge began by standing and saying, "Well, folks, I've received orders, and I thought you might like to know where we're going." He gestured at a star map on the wall across from the ports. "We'll be going to Morlandria. Have any of you ever been there?"

"Yes sir, I was there once." Bronwen Llewellen was still attractive at fifty-two. She was small and had silver hair and dark blue eyes.

Bronwen had a long history with space exploration. On his first mission, Edge had been reluctant to take an older woman, but she was the aunt of Dai Bando, and Dai Bando would not go unless his aunt was included. And Mei-Lani would not go unless Dai Bando went . . . It had been a complicated affair. But many times Edge had been glad that Bronwen Llewellen was on board. Not only was she was a splendid navigator, but the woman's Christianity fascinated him.

Now it was the dark-haired Dai who asked, "What was it like on Morlandria, Aunt?"

Dai was not a scientist or even mechanically inclined, but he was invaluable in any task calling for physical strength or agility. He possessed exceptional skills in that area and was faster than anyone Mark Edge had ever seen. So far the boy had even been able to avoid defeat by Weapons Officer Tara Jaleel, who was a specialist in the martial arts.

"It's a fine planet," the navigator said. "Very beautiful indeed, and there are many things to do there that you'll all enjoy. The beaches are especially beautiful."

"Well," Heck Jordan said, "if it was me, I'd rather be going to where we could make some money. Like back to Makon."

"Will you hush, Heck!" Raina St. Clair dug her elbow into Heck's side. "Don't you ever think about anything but money?"

"Yes, I do. I think about food, and—" he reached over and tried to take her hand "—and I think about partying. Mostly about me and you."

Ignoring their bickering, Edge said, "I'm sure we'll get a tough mission soon enough."

"So how about a mission back to Makon?" The irrepressible Heck spoke up again. "If we could just get back there, we'd *all* be rich."

The *Daystar*'s first mission had been to the planet Makon. There Edge had found large deposits of tridium, a remarkable gemstone that was harder than diamonds and found on Makon only. The mission had not worked out the way he had planned, but Heck Jordan never gave up trying to get the captain to take the *Daystar* back. No one knew how to get to Makon except Captain Edge. And that information was sought after by the wily Sir Richard Irons and had almost cost them their lives.

"Not this time, Heck," Edge said. "I think we need a little R and R after our last mission. Anything else?"

There was nothing else, and the meeting was adjourned.

Jerusha walked down the corridor, and Heck followed her. He was loudly complaining about losing money by not cornering the market in tridium. At the same time he was trying to hold her hand.

"Keep your grubby hands to yourself, Heck! Don't you ever get tired of trying to be the great lover?"

"Can't help it." Heck grinned. "I got to be me."

"Well, you are obnoxious!"

"Aw, you're just putting on an act. You know you're really falling for me."

Heck seemed to have the skin of a rhinoceros. No matter how many times he was rebuffed, he remained convinced he was the world's greatest Romeo.

Jerusha suddenly faced him. "Don't you ever think about the Lord, Heck?"

All the other Rangers were Christians, and Heck often said he had heard more than enough sermons.

"A fellow's got to make his own way."

"No, that's not true. None of us can make our own way, as you put it. It takes the Lord to help us."

"I'm not buying it. I'm smart, and I've got lots of opportunities coming up."

"But who made you smart, Heck?"

"I was born that way."

"You were born that way, and you're intelligent because God made you so," Jerusha insisted. She spoke out of a good heart. She herself was very competitive. She hated to lose at anything and was really a very tough young lady. But God had done a work in her, and she was truly concerned about this boy who apparently never thought of anything but himself.

"Money is where it's at," Heck concluded.

"No, money is not the only thing."

The two had reached Heck's station. He was continuing to argue that he didn't need God or anything else when suddenly he broke off, exclaiming, "Jerusha, look at that!"

Her gaze, like Heck Jordan's, fixed on the view screen. "What's *that?*"

"It's a ship, and it's headed straight for us!"

Heck's hands flew over the controls in front of him, and, indeed, he was a very able young man even if he was obnoxious. "I've got the registry here. Look, it's an Intergalactic Academy P54 Combat Convette!"

"What does all that mean?" Jerusha demanded.

"It means," Heck said thoughtfully, "it's about the hottest ship flying out of the Intergalactic Academy. We'd better let the captain know. No telling what is going on with that kind of hot rod chasing us down!"

3

Faces from the Past

Contact established with P54, sir!"

From her console, Raina St. Clair glanced at the view screen and then shot a look toward Jerusha Ericson, who stood to the right of the captain's station.

Jerusha said nothing, but she stood ramrod straight and kept her eyes fixed on the screen as memories of her days at the Intergalactic Academy came flooding back.

Karl and Olga, she thought. *I thought we had seen the last of them—at least, I hoped we had seen the last of them!*

It had been Karl Bentlow and Olga Von Kemp who had made life miserable for her. The two had been the favorites of the director of the Academy, Commander Marta Inch. To begin with, Inch hated the cadets who professed to follow Christ, and she had done all she could to get them out of the Academy. She also had been highly successful. Ringo, Mei-Lani, and Jerusha had all been expelled on very unstable grounds.

Now Jerusha studied the two faces on the screen and tried to stem the anger that rushed through her.

"Captain Edge of the cruiser *Daystar.* Identify yourself."

The young man on the view screen spoke first. He was almost indecently handsome, having dark auburn hair, cornflower blue eyes, and lashes long enough to be the envy of a girl. He had a straight, English nose, and when he smiled, as he did now, a dimple appeared on each cheek. "Ensign Karl Bentlow of the Inter-galactic Fleet, Captain Edge," he said. His voice was overconfident to the point of arrogance.

Then, before Bentlow could say more, the girl spoke up. "I'm surprised to see you're still under way." Olga Von Kemp was short and had rather masculine features. She wore her straight brown hair clipped short, her brown eyes had a hard glint, and there was a smirk in her voice as she added, "I never expected the *Daystar* to prove operative. Congratulations. You suc-ceeded in spite of what everyone in space is calling the Nursery Crew."

Since Olga Von Kemp was fifteen herself and Karl Bentlow sixteen, the reference to the ages of the Space Rangers was not valid. Nevertheless, Captain Edge lift-ed his head and glanced briefly at Jerusha.

She assumed he was remembering some of the things she had told him about Olga and Karl. He wouldn't want any rivalry going on during a flight.

"What is your business in the area?"

"We're on special assignment, Captain," Karl said.

"You're invading our airspace. I suggest you pull your ship away."

"You don't have to worry, Captain. We could fly rings around that antique you're flying."

Edge frowned, and for a moment he made no reply. Jerusha knew there was just enough truth in Karl Bentlow's remark to irritate him but at the same time make him cautious.

It was true enough that the P54 Combat Convette that kept its station alongside the *Daystar* was a supe-rior ship. For one thing, the P54 was twice the size of the *Daystar 831-B*.

Edge's ship was shaped more conventionally. It was similar to a rocket with wings. The P54, on the other hand, was a circular-style cruiser, built some-what like a flying saucer. This design enabled the P54 to perform course changes that would tear the *Daystar* apart. Galactic Command had also invented an improved system for controlling inertia, which allowed the P54 crew to withstand the "G forces" during ultra-quick course changes.

Yes, Karl Bentlow's comment would make Captain Edge wary.

As the conversation between the captain and the Convette went on, Ringo Smith murmured to Mei-Lani, standing beside him, "Why did *those* two have to appear?"

"I wouldn't be surprised but what Karl intercepted us just on account of Jerusha."

Ringo gaped at her. "Aw, come on! He wouldn't be crazy enough to do that!"

"Yes," Mei-Lani said, nodding, "he would. He was always crazy about her, and now he's just showing off."

"Well," Ringo grumbled, "they must be getting senile at the Intergalactic Council to trust a Convette to Karl Bentlow."

"Yeah," Heck said. "I don't think he can even ride a bicycle real good."

Actually, that part was not true, as Heck was well aware. Karl Bentlow had been one of the Academy's star pupils. But he and Olga had made so much fun of Heck that he despised them.

"I wish Lieutenant Jaleel would give them a little blast from a laser cannon," he muttered. "Nothing serious —just enough to blow them up, you understand."

The conversation between the captain and the two intruders was growing prickly. Karl and Olga took turns making fun of the *Daystar*, its lack of speed and firepower. Olga made continual slighting remarks about the crew as well, and, although she did not mention names, Jerusha knew exactly at whom her barbed remarks were directed.

On impulse Jerusha stepped from her station to Captain Edge's side, staring up at the view screen. She assumed that her face was pale. She certainly knew that anger sparked in her eyes.

"Karl, you and Olga can blast off anytime you feel like it!" she told them. Her voice was not quite steady, as if she was close to losing control. "We got this far without your help, and we don't need anything from you!"

"Why, hello, Jerusha," Karl said. He smiled, and Jerusha could not help but admit he still looked like a movie star. "It's good to see you again."

Olga Von Kemp gave a short, jealous glance at Karl, then turned her eyes back on Jerusha. "Surprised to see you've found work. Most people, after they get expelled from the Academy for incompetence, have great difficulty. But I guess no matter how incompetent people are, they can always find something."

A fresh surge of anger poured through Jerusha. She hated to lose at anything, and she had always felt that she had lost when she allowed herself to get expelled. Somehow Karl and Olga had become a symbol of her own failure. Her voice rose sharply as she said, "We don't need you in this area! State your business and then get out!"

"Jerusha—" Captain Edge put his hand gently on her arm. "You forget yourself. Take your station."

"That's right, Captain," Olga said. "She's always like that." The girl grinned. "Always wanting to run everything and not competent. Go on, Jerusha. Why don't you go to your room?"

All this time, Contessa had been standing by the bulkhead. Suddenly the German shepherd, a dog specially bred for superintelligence, seemed to interpret what was happening on the view screen as a threat to her mistress.

Or perhaps she remembered the time when this very one on the screen had come upon her, tied and waiting for Jerusha, who had left the dog for a few moments. Olga had tormented Contessa, who could not break loose, finally even beating her severely.

In any case, without a sound, Contessa—a streak of black fur—launched herself at the screen. Her one hundred eighty pounds struck the viewer, and instantly it turned blank.

"Raina! Quick! Get that picture back!" Edge yelled. "Jerusha, take that animal off the bridge!"

The picture was restored at once, and Edge said, "Captain Edge here. We don't need you in this area. Signing off." He nodded at Raina, who, with one stroke of her finger, canceled the communication.

Looking out the window, they all watched as the Convette applied power and left the *Daystar* behind as if she were standing still.

The P54's departure was almost faster than Jerusha's eye could follow. "To think, I could have been assigned on one of those."

"If getting there means rejecting Jesus," Raina reminded her, "there's not a ship in the galaxy that's worth having!"

"I know, Raina, but I dreamed about being on a P54 for a long time."

"So did I, but it was a dream that both of us were forced to let go. God has a purpose in everything. He has one in this too. You'll see. You'll thank the Lord you didn't wind up on one of those!"

Dr. Temple Cole lifted the head of crewman Simms, who had managed to get himself hit on the head in the cargo hold. "Simms," she said, "you may have a concussion." Holding up two fingers, she said, "How many fingers do you see?"

"Five." Simms nodded happily. He was a hulking man with exceptional physical strength but little better than average intelligence.

"Five? You see five?"

"Yep, I do," Simms said. "You're holding two up, two down, and your thumb's behind them two. That makes five."

Disgusted, Dr. Cole shook her head. Sighing deeply, she straightened up. "Go on back to your quarters and try to stay out of the way of anything falling."

"Chief Cagney told me," Simms said as he headed for the door, "if anything else fell to make sure it hit my head. Said it wouldn't hurt me if I got hit there. Pretty funny, huh?"

"Very funny. Now go along, Simms."

Temple Cole turned back into her office area and went about her desk work with smooth efficiency. She was five-feet-five inches and twenty-seven years old, but looked younger. Her strawberry blonde hair was cut short but still had a rebellious curl. Her violet eyes were her most unusual feature, and she was more shapely than most flight surgeons on starships in the Intergalactic Fleet. As she worked steadily at her filing, she kept thinking of the scene that had taken place up on the bridge.

Her eyes had been fixed on Jerusha's face during the episode before the view screen, and all afternoon she had thought about the girl. Abruptly she turned from the file cabinet and touched the communicator on her belt. "Dr. Cole to Jerusha Ericson," she said. "Report to surgery at once."

Five minutes later, Jerusha entered. The girl looked apprehensive. "You wanted to see me, Dr. Cole?"

Seeing her flushed face, Temple said quickly, "I'm sorry, Jerusha. I didn't mean for it to sound quite so urgent. Come in and sit down."

"I really can't be away from my station too long . . ."

"This won't take long. Would you have something to drink?"

"No, thank you."

"I believe I'll have some juice. We just got this new melon nectar from the planet Netan. I've never tasted anything like it—it's sort of a combination of watermelon, peach, and a soft drink. Why don't you try it?" Dr. Cole insisted, more for the purpose of calming the girl down than out of politeness. She was obviously still tense.

The two sat, and, as Jerusha gradually relaxed, Temple said as innocently as she could, "That was quite a thing on the bridge this morning—Contessa jumping at that screen."

"It was because Olga always tormented her at the Academy. She still remembers her. It's a good thing she wasn't really here."

"I should think so. Contessa is unusually smart and very loyal. She would be quite a handful." Temple took a sip of her drink, then said, "I take it you and Olga weren't good friends."

"You could safely say that. Or you might even say we hated each other."

"What was the primary problem?"

A hard look came into the ensign's eyes. "Olga always hated anyone that did better than she did on exercises. And it wasn't just me. But . . . there was something else." She hesitated, lowering her eyes. Then looking up again, she shrugged. "She's always been in love with Karl Bentlow, and when he tried to date me, that infuriated her."

"So. She's a woman scorned. Well, they can be dangerous. I've had some experience along that line." The doctor smiled and swirled the amber-colored juice around in her glass. She took another sip, then said, "So why do I think there's still more to this than you're telling me? It's not *just* a matter of her being jealous over Bentlow, is it?"

"No, it's not," the girl admitted. "Commander Inch always hated any cadets who were Christians, and she did everything she could to get us expelled. Well, she got the job done, and it was Olga who gave her the ammunition to do it with. I've had a hard time forgiving her for that!"

"I can understand." The surgeon stared into space. Some past bitterness of her own was coming back to fill her mind.

Perhaps something in Dr. Cole's voice caught Jerusha's attention. Her head came up. "You had something like this happen to you, didn't you, Dr. Cole?"

"Well, I suppose most of us have experienced betrayal at one time or other."

Temple sighed. Her last ship had been lost with almost all hands. The captain was the one who was responsible. He had also been in love with her, or so he had said. Nevertheless, at the court-martial he had thrown all the guilt on her, and she had lost her place in the star fleet. Suddenly she wanted to tell Jerusha all this, but then decided that it would be useless to do so. She had called in the girl in order to help *her*. Why did she now feel that their positions had reversed?

Jerusha said quietly, "I have struggled forgiving Olga, but I've done it. It wasn't easy, but I've found out one thing, Dr. Cole. Unforgiveness and hard feelings hurt the one who holds them much more than they hurt the one they are directed against."

"I know that's what you believe. It's a biblical teaching, isn't it?"

"Yes, it is. The Scripture just says forgive others as Christ has forgiven you. It's that simple."

Jerusha sat talking quietly with the flight surgeon far longer than she had intended. But by the time she left surgery, she felt that some sort of healing had taken place in her own heart. It often happened that way. Thoughts of past injuries would come, she would flare up inwardly, and then she would realize that as a Christian she could not afford to act in such a way.

I hope Dr. Cole is able to forgive whoever it was that hurt her, she thought as she walked down the corridor. *If she doesn't, she'll be in real trouble.*

For a while after Jerusha left, Temple Cole moved around her quarters restlessly, not really working but thinking of the girl. She turned when a tap came at the door and it opened.

Temple smiled at her unexpected visitor. "Hello, Mei-Lani." She liked the young oriental girl very much. "You don't have a flu bug, do you?"

But a strange expression came into Mei-Lani's eyes. She stopped where she was and seemed to be speechless.

The distress in those dark brown eyes was unusual. "What is it? *Are* you sick?"

"No . . . no, I'm fine."

"Is something else troubling you, then?"

For one moment Mei-Lani seemed about ready to speak. She stood on the brink, it appeared, ready to say what it was that brought that unhappy expression to her eyes. But then, with an abrupt shake of her head, she said, "No, it's nothing, really." And she started for the door, almost running.

"Mei-Lani, wait—" But the girl was gone, and Dr. Cole's shoulders sagged. *Now what's wrong with her? Could be anything. Thirteen-year-old girls think they've got all the troubles of the world on their shoulders.*

She thought for a minute and tried to smile. *And it doesn't get much better for twenty-seven-year-old girls!*

4

Arrival at Memphis

The dining hall was filled to capacity, and the air was full of laughter as the *Daystar* crew enjoyed a fine dinner prepared by Manta, the flight cook.

Manta was a small—almost dwarfish—man from the planet Skeizar. Manta was his first name. When asked his last name, he always responded with a look of disdain. "Nobody on Skeizar has a second name," he would say. "For the simple reason that nobody ever uses the same first name. There was only one Manta on the whole planet, and that was me! Dumb, if you ask me, to use the same name as somebody else!"

Manta was irritable and not an easy man to deal with, but he was a wonderful cook. This evening he had outdone himself.

The meal consisted of rock kidneys from the planet Bealor, steak marinated in a light sauce tasting something like mushrooms, crisp colorful salad with fresh greens and exotic flowers from the planet Merlina, and a clear soup made from the roots of vegetables grown on Ciephus. That tasted like a cross between carrots and red beets. Then there were large and odd-looking vegetables with unusual flavors, and a creamy dessert filled with brightly colored fruit.

Heck Jordan, who loved eating as well as any man in the galaxy, shoveled down portions of the pudding. It was made from a foreign grain that tasted like nothing he had ever eaten before. He was wearing garish clothes tonight, as he always did when off duty and sometimes when on. His trousers were a startling shade of orange, his jersey was purplish, and he had a pale green cloth tied around his head.

Heck finally paused long enough to gasp, "You just wait until we get to Morlandria. It's going to be a blast. I hear the planet's a tourist paradise."

"So I hear, too," Studs Cagney said. Tonight the crew chief wore a new white shirt that bulged with the heavy muscles of his arms and chest. Now he winked at Heck. "Why don't you and me go around and hit some of the clubs they got in the capital? They say they're pretty spicy."

"Is that right?" Heck grinned. Then he winked at Raina and said, "So what do you say, sweetie? You want to go with me and the chief?"

"I don't think so," Raina said quietly. "From what the chief says, those clubs are not places that I ought to be—or want to be."

"Well," Tara Jaleel said huffily, "there's no point in being a fanatic."

Lieutenant Jaleel was without doubt the most spectacular-appearing officer on the ship. Of African descent, she came from the tall Masai people, and she was almost six feet. The weapons officer had attractive and clear-cut features, but there was a fierce manner about her. Like her far distant ancestors, Tara Jaleel was bloodthirsty and loved battle of any kind.

But then she gave Raina a tight smile and said, "I'll even go with you, and if anybody gives you any trouble, I'll take care of it."

"I guess if Dai is with me, I won't have any trouble," Raina said. "But thank you." She felt strongly that the older woman—Tara Jaleel was actually only twenty-four—was a bad influence on the crew. The weapons officer was truly a pagan and resented Christianity with a passion.

Tara Jaleel glared at Raina and then cut her eyes toward Dai Bando, sitting farther down the table. The young man was eating quietly and was engaged in conversation with Zeno Thrax. Apparently he had not heard what was going on. So far, Dai Bando was the only person that Tara Jaleel could not defeat in Jai-Kando, the ancient form of martial arts that she took such pleasure in.

Zeno Thrax had extraordinary hearing. Besides, he seemed also to have the ability to listen in on at least five conversations at the same time. He glanced at Lieutenant Jaleel but said nothing. He was well aware —as was everyone else—that the lieutenant was dissatisfied with the youthful Rangers. Actually, Zeno had found them to be delightful company.

"Why don't you and I do some exploring together, Dai?" he asked the boy.

"Why, I'd like that, First!" Dai said pleasantly. He was flattered, for Zeno Thrax did not mix easily with the rest of the crew.

Dai recognized that the first officer was lonely, and he'd heard the rumor that Zeno was, for some reason, cut off from his people. The man had apparently done something that was taboo on his home planet, and he had been exiled.

But Dai would not ask questions. He did like Zeno, however. The albino had a keen sense of humor, and he loved games.

"What are *you* going to do on Morlandria, Mei-Lani?" Ringo asked. He was sitting across from Mei-Lani and at the same time was keeping his eye on Raina St. Clair.

Mei-Lani saw that Ringo was not really listening

for her answer, but she answered anyway. "I'm going to make a journey to an ancient shrine."

"A shrine? What kind of a shrine?" Ringo asked, turning to face her, his interest captured.

"It's way deep in the jungle. I found the history of the place, and there was even a map showing how to get there." Actually, she had stayed up late at night searching for the information on the computer and had printed it out.

"Why would you want to go to a place like that?" Ringo asked, a puzzled expression on his face. "It sounds to me like it would be more fun to go into the capital. Be lots of things going on there."

Mei-Lani toyed with the steak that was set before her. She cut it into tiny pieces and then speared a morsel. "Well, my parents visited this shrine when they were on their honeymoon. They were on a planet-hopping trip. Visited about six, I think, and Morlandria was one of them."

"So now you want to go back there. Did they show you pictures of the place?"

"Why, yes. They did. And they kept saying there was something very strange about the place. They wouldn't go into it, but it made me curious. Would you like to go with me, Ringo?"

"No, thanks, Mei-Lani. I've got other things on my mind."

In the exercise room, Tara Jaleel adjusted her sparring outfit and looked up with surprise. She was wearing a loose-fitting white uniform and had been awaiting her next student—or victim, as the Space Rangers preferred to call themselves. In this case it would be Heck Jordan. Captain Edge required all of the

Rangers to take Jai-Kando lessons, and most of them hated the experience thoroughly. All except Dai Bando.

But here came Ringo Smith, and he was certainly not one of the crew who enjoyed her lessons in Jai-Kando.

"Well, Smith, what can I do for you? You want another lesson?"

"No, thanks, Lieutenant. I'm still bruised from the last one."

"Pain is good for you." Tara nodded seriously. She sincerely meant this, and she herself could bear pain without showing any sign whatsoever. "Well, I'm sure you didn't come down to socialize."

"Why, I might, Lieutenant. You never know. I'm interested in some of the things you do."

"Like what?" Lieutenant Jaleel asked suspiciously.

"Well, to tell the truth, you've been around a lot, and you're a woman, and I want to get a woman's point of view."

"About what?"

The direct question seemed to fluster Ringo. He shifted nervously from one foot to the other. Then he shrugged his shoulders. "I'm interested in a girl, and she's not really interested in me."

Tara Jaleel did not smile often, but now she did. Then she laughed aloud. "Do you think I'm one of those columnists that write about how to win the love of your sweetheart?"

"Well, no, not really, but I've tried everything, Lieutenant. And I need help." Ringo's voice was filled with despair. He fingered the medallion that hung from his neck and then blurted out, "Well, I guess the truth is that I don't know very much about love. Just what I've read about and seen in films. And this girl—I really like her."

41

"I don't know why you don't name her. Everyone knows you're crazy over Raina St. Clair."

A blush tinged Ringo's cheeks, and he nodded. "Well, that's true, but I can't get anywhere with her. She just won't pay me any mind. Sometimes I think she can't see anybody but Dai Bando."

Instantly the humor left Tara Jaleel's face. Her eyes narrowed to slits. Lieutenant Jaleel did not like Dai Bando, the only man—or woman, for that matter—who had ever bested her. And he only sixteen at that.

"So, you think your lover is interested in Dai? Well, that is interesting. What have you done to attract her attention?"

She listened as Ringo related the efforts he had made. When he had finished, she wagged her head. "That's no good. No good at all. I don't like Bando, but you'll have to admit he is a good-looking young man."

"I know it. And he can sing too! What can *I* do? Nothing but run a computer! That's not going to impress anybody!"

"No, likely it isn't, but I know something that will."

"You do? What is it? Can I use it?"

"I think you can, Smith. Come with me." She walked to the end of the gymnasium, where she opened an intricately carved walnut cabinet.

"Here," she said, stepping aside. "This is what will help you."

Ringo stared at the small statue that stood inside the cabinet.

"What's *that?*" he asked fearfully.

"It is Sheva. She has tremendous power."

"It's an idol? I couldn't have anything to do with that!" Ringo was not a strong Christian believer, but he knew better than to have anything to do with an idol.

"Oh, don't be foolish! This is just a *replica* of

Sheva. The real Sheva cannot be reduced to a piece of wood or brass or gold. Of course not. Here—come over here and sit down. Let me tell you some of the things that Sheva has done for me."

Rather reluctantly Ringo sat on a bench beside Tara Jaleel.

The weapons office began to talk, and her voice became softer than he had ever heard it. In spite of himself, Ringo was fascinated by the tales that she told. She had certainly led an exciting life. As she told of facing certain death time after time and then being saved from it by Sheva, her goddess, Ringo found himself growing more and more interested.

Still, when she finished, he said, "Well, I don't know, Lieutenant." A worried frown wrinkled his brow. "I really don't need anything like *that* for my problem. All I want is to make a girl fall in love with me."

"That can be arranged. Now listen very carefully. Here is what you must do . . ."

The *Daystar* was cruising near the capital of Morlandria.

"That's Memphis right there," Captain Edge said, pointing out the city to Temple Cole.

"It's a pretty place. In fact, it's a beautiful planet."

"Yes, it seems to be. I don't know much about it. I do know some strange things have happened here."

"What kind of strange things?" Temple looked up at him. "What do you mean, 'strange'?"

"Well, I don't fully understand. But people who have been here say there's something a little bit mystical about this place. Something about the gods of the local people. But no one talks about it much."

They watched as the *Daystar* circled, preparing for landing. Morlandria *was* beautiful. Its orbit around its sun enabled the planet to have springlike weather year round. From space, the planet looked much like Earth, except that there were no frozen poles or arid deserts. The continents were a luscious green, spangled with purple mountaintops and large blue lakes. The valleys contained clear rivers. White sand beaches surrounded Morlandria's three oceans.

Edge wondered how anything sinister could exist in a place with so much beauty.

"Plot a course to Memphis," he ordered.

"Captain," Bronwen Llewellen reported as she continued adjusting the navigation controls, "the Memphis Space Port Authority has assigned us to docking port twelve."

In a few moments they were approaching the space port. Edge could see that many luxury cruisers were already docked.

"And look there!" Raina said, pointing to port eight. "There's the P54!"

"Just my luck!" Jerusha's eyes snapped.

Raina smiled. "Well, you have to admit that the P54 looks wonderful. What a ship!"

As Jerusha glared at her, Edge said, "OK, you two, this trip is not about Bentlow, Von Kemp, or the Intergalactic Academy. We're here for R and R. Now forget the P54. It's just a ship."

Raina and Jerusha looked at each other and started to laugh. Then they look back at the captain. "Aye, aye, sir!" They saluted Edge and ran off the bridge into the corridor, giggling in anticipation of their vacation.

These are good kids! Edge thought. *Someday I'll have to confront that Commander Inch. She has no idea the hurt that she has caused them.*

The *Daystar* extended its atmospheric stabilizers and soared in a wide arc toward the Memphis space port. Once the ship was aligned with docking port twelve, Edge dropped the landing gear, and the cruiser floated to a graceful landing.

Captain Edge suddenly said to Temple Cole, "How about you and I exploring some of the city, Temple?"

At the touch of his hand on her arm, the ship's doctor looked up and gave him a smile. "All right, Captain. I think that would be nice."

Soon most of the eager crew was lining up, all chattering happily. Then they piled out of the *Daystar* and headed for their leave in Memphis.

It was Ringo Smith who brought up the rear. His eyes were on Tara Jaleel, who gave him a meaningful glance. She did not speak, but Ringo nodded, and this seemed to please the lieutenant.

5

Duke Zeigler

M ei-Lani, I think you ought to go with us and enjoy yourself in the city."

Mei-Lani was in Jerusha's cabin borrowing a jacket to wear in the thick jungle that she planned to visit.

Jerusha was arranging her hair and studying her reflection in the mirror. Now she cocked her head to one side and leaned forward into the glass. "I wonder if I ought to start wearing more eye makeup?"

"Oh, I don't think so," Mei-Lani answered. "You look nice just like you are." She picked up the blue nylon jacket that Jerusha had given her and slipped into it. It was too big, of course. Jerusha was a tall, Scandinavian type at five feet ten inches, and Mei-Lani was barely more than five feet. But she turned up the sleeves and said, "This will do fine. Thank you."

"And I certainly don't think you ought to go alone!" Jerusha argued. She fluffed her hair with her fingers, then turned from the mirror to her young friend. "Who knows? There could be dangerous animals out there! Don't you remember some of those monsters we ran into on other planets?" She shivered. "If it hadn't been for Dai Bando that one time, I could have been eaten alive!"

"Oh, it'll be all right. I'll take my Neuromag with me. But I can't imagine that this planet would have anything really dangerous living on it. After all, Morlandria is a *tourist* planet."

Jerusha seemed unconvinced, and she scowled

47

her disapproval. "Mei-Lani, look at yourself. You're so small! I can just imagine a large bird of prey picking you up, flying you to its nest, and having you for supper!"

With an abrupt knock, the door opened, admitting Bronwen Llewellen. Bronwen was wearing heavy-duty clothes, including a dark green canvas tunic and trousers that extended down to the boots on her feet. "Zeno and I have decided that we are going with you on this expedition, Mei-Lani," she said and smiled warmly.

In the corridor behind Bronwen, Mei-Lani glimpsed First Officer Zeno Thrax.

Zeno, also, was wearing canvas clothing, and Mei-Lani noted the heavy-duty Neuromag holstered on his belt. "I've seen enough cities, but I'm always interested in the flora and fauna of any new world," he said.

"Flora and fauna? What's that?" Jerusha asked, puzzled.

"Oh, the vegetation and the animals." Zeno's pale eyes gleamed with humor.

No doubt he had really been planning to spend his R and R time on the ship, Mei-Lani thought. And then Bronwen Llewellen, upon hearing that Mei-Lani was exploring the ruins of an ancient shrine, had approached him and asked him to go along for protection.

Zeno stood in the doorway, patting the Neuromag. "I doubt if there would be anything out there that could stand up to this weapon."

"Well, then I feel better," Jerusha said, approval in her dark blue eyes. "I've been telling Mei-Lani she needs a bodyguard."

"You may not have known, Mei-Lani, but Captain Edge was going to refuse your request," Bronwen said. "He said it was too risky to go alone, and he was right."

Mei-Lani smiled. "I'm glad you're both going. It's going to be exciting."

"What are you actually expecting to find?" Bronwen inquired.

Since Mei-Lani Lao was the historian as well as the linguist on board the *Daystar*, she had an answer ready. "Let me tell you about the shrine," she said excitedly.

"What kind of shrine is it?" Zeno asked.

"If you'll be patient, Zeno—" Bronwen smiled "—we'll hear it. Go ahead, Mei-Lani."

Mei-Lani's eyes lit up, happy that Zeno and Bronwen were interested in something that was so important to her. "I guess my thirst for history was passed down to me by my parents." She thought of her childhood. "Even when I was very little, they used to talk about their honeymoon on Morlandria. Of course, there were many pleasurable things to do on the planet, then as now. One day they chose to visit the Shrine of Ugarit."

"What is Ugarit, and why does Ugarit need a shrine?" Zeno asked.

"Will you be quiet and let Mei-Lani tell her story?" Bronwen interjected.

Mei-Lani went on. "My parents were archeologists. They actually met each other at a dig on Earth. The dig was in the ancient land of Canaan at a place called Ugarit. Ugarit was also called Ras Shamra. The place had been a great commercial and religious center in the days of old." Mei-Lani hoped that she wasn't being long-winded. "Anyway, my parents were involved with this dig in Ugarit, and they discovered a hidden room underneath this shrine called 'The Stairs of Ashtaroth.' And what they saw in that room changed their lives." Mei-Lani fell silent.

Bronwen smoothed the wrinkles from her heavy tunic. After a moment she said, "Mei-Lani, tell us what they saw."

"They went into this room. It was very dusty, so my father took his brush and cleared the dust off a wall, and there was a carving of a beautiful woman standing at a window. Underneath the woman was the inscription 'Ashtaroth—goddess of Morlandria.' It was a great find, and it gave my parents quite a reputation with archeologists."

"So how does that fit in with *this* shrine?" Thrax asked.

"After that, my parents went searching for the ancient city of Morlandria. They looked for a long time, but like everyone before them, they couldn't locate where the city had been. Then, about fourteen years ago, they married and decided to spend their honeymoon on a planet they'd read about in a space travel magazine."

Zeno's albino eyes opened wide. "A planet named Morlandria!"

"That's right—Morlandria. The whole coincidence was too compelling for my parents. Anyway, they came to this planet and visited the local shrine at Ugarit. There were beautiful pictures and inscriptions engraved on the walls everywhere, but what they saw also horrified them."

Mei-Lani stopped a moment to compose her thoughts. "On this planet, Ashtaroth is called Astarte—the same name the Greeks gave Ashtaroth! How could a planet thousands of light-years away from Earth have a goddess with the same name as an ancient goddess on Earth? Well, that night they discovered that Astarte was more than just a name for an ancient goddess. Astarte—rather, the power behind Astarte—was real."

"So you're telling me they *saw* a goddess, a real goddess in the flesh?" Thrax asked incredulously.

"All at once they started hearing drums and chanting underneath them in the shrine. They finally found a tunnel that led farther underground to a big cave. There was a large stone altar in the center of the cave, and the place was filled with people, wildly running all around. It was scary. My parents were good people. They introduced me to the Lord when I was very young. They truly saw terrifying things happen in the Shrine of Ugarit that day. They didn't make up the story."

"This sounds terrifying, Mei-Lani! Why would you even want to visit this place?" Bronwen asked.

Thrax's curiosity was getting the best of him. "Did they tell you anything else?"

"I know you'll find this hard to believe, but they said they saw some sort of scary vision or whatever it was. Then the chanting got louder, and people screamed, and my parents—fearing for their lives—ran back up the tunnel to the surface. They left Morlandria as soon as possible."

Bronwen nodded her head in agreement. "That was a very smart thing for your parents to do."

"On their way back to Earth, they happened to meet a Christian man. They told him what they'd seen in the cave, and he said that they had probably seen a manifestation of a powerful servant of Satan—Astarte, or Ashtaroth, who is also called the 'Queen of Heaven.' He explained to them that some people are deceived into believing that she is the goddess of love, and artists have painted beautiful pictures of her. But the truth is that Astarte's beauty is a deception. Actually, she is a very powerful wicked spirit, who seeks to destroy God's people."

Mei-Lani picked up her Bible. "That's when he told them about Jesus—that He was the only protection anybody had from Satan's power. Well, after what my parents had witnessed, they were more than ready to be introduced to Jesus Christ, and they became very committed Christians. Then the man gave them this Bible. My father carried it with him everywhere. Before he . . . died . . . my father gave his Bible to me."

"How did your father die?" Thrax asked softly.

With tears in her eyes, Mei-Lani looked straight into Zeno Thrax's colorless face. "I can't share that right now. Maybe someday, Zeno, but not right now."

Bronwen put a comforting arm around Mei-Lani as Zeno asked, "And what do you know about the shrine today?"

Mei-Lani looked at him while returning Bronwen's hug. "From what I've researched in the library computer, the Shrine of Ugarit hasn't been used for hundreds of years. It's almost covered with bushes, trees, and vines. In fact, we may not be able to find it at all."

Then she wiped her tears from her face. "But because of what happened to my parents, I've got to find the Shrine of Ugarit. And who knows if I'll ever be on Morlandria again?"

"Well, it sounds more exciting than going to any city," Zeno said matter-of-factly. "I'm ready if you ladies are."

Mei-Lani found that Zeno had assembled the *Daystar*'s all-terrain Land Rover. One of the grunts had written in dust the name "Bone-Crusher" across the hood. It was a very functional vehicle but offered little comfort.

Mei-Lani waved at Jerusha as they began their expedition.

Jerusha waved good-bye. Then she turned back to the cruiser and immediately encountered Dai Bando, his black hair gleaming in the sunshine.

He smiled a greeting and said, "Hello, Jerusha. You ready for a wild time in town?"

"Nothing like that," Jerusha said. She liked the young Welshman very much. "Have you seen Captain Edge?"

"Yes. He took off by himself. I heard the first officer ask him where he was going, and he was just real mysterious about it."

Jerusha thought for a moment and then said with a laugh, "I wonder if he's going into town looking for a girlfriend."

"Why should he do that when he has Temple Cole?" Dai asked innocently. "He's real stuck on the doctor, you know."

Giving him a disgusted look, Jerusha shook her head but only murmured under her breath, "Boys sure don't have much judgment!"

As she made her way with Heck and Ivan Petroski into Memphis, Jerusha wondered what sort of girl Captain Mark Edge *was* looking for. *He's good-looking enough to get any girl he wants*, she thought. Somehow that thought disturbed her, and she had to force herself to join in their light talk as they entered the city.

As Mark Edge walked through the streets of the capital, he kept the flap on his holster open. It was not that he expected any danger, but a lifetime of living on the edge of it had made him very much aware. He had developed a certain sixth sense—almost like an extra set of eyes and ears—so that, when something threatening was near, he seemed to smell it or see it or hear it. One sure sign was that the hair on the back of his neck would rise up.

However, he did not sense any threats today. He ambled along, looking at the low buildings. They appeared to be made of marble, but when he touched one it gave way under his hand, so he knew he was wrong about that. Most were little more than three or four stories high, and he wondered why there were no skyscrapers in Memphis.

The inhabitants, he decided, were rather garden variety. He had been on some planets where the citizens were startling—extremely tall or small or having odd coloration such as the dwellers on the red planet where even the children were a crimson hue. But the people in Memphis looked to be just ordinary people going about their work—some obviously just more wealthy than others.

Captain Edge had a map etched inside his head, and he had learned to follow maps very well. As he came to a certain side street he thought for a moment, then strode down the narrow alley. It dead-ended at a closed door.

He looked for a bell but found none. So he lifted his fist and beat on the door, then stepped back to await the results.

The door opened cautiously, but then it was thrown wide, and a tall man as skinny as a snake came out. He had a grin on his thin face and a light in his pale blue eyes.

"Well, Mark Edge! The longer they come, the uglier they get!" he said. He threw his long arms around Mark and gave him a rough hug, then hit him on the shoulder with a fist before stepping back. "I been waitin' for you. What did you have to do—go all the way to Jupiter to get here?"

"You always were an impatient guy, Duke."

He stepped inside at the other man's invitation, remembering the sort of experiences that he had had with Duke Zeigler. Some of them he didn't really want to remember.

"What are you up to these days, Duke? Nothing legal, I'm sure."

"Aw, come on, Mark. You know me. I'm a straight arrow."

"Yes, I know all about that. Come on. Level with me."

"Have you eaten yet?"

"No. I'm starved, as a matter of fact."

"Then let me throw something together for you."

Zeigler seated him at a round table with a black marble top and began taking things out of a cabinet. The man had always been a marvelous cook—one of his many talents—Mark thought.

As Duke prepared the meal, he talked about old times and soon had his visitor laughing.

Mark had always liked Zeigler, despite the man's shady reputation and background. And as Duke began setting dishes before him, he thought, *Well, I'm afraid I was once as crooked as he was. Just barely managed to stay out of jail. I suspect Duke hasn't changed much. I hope I have.*

"Sink your teeth into this. It's kangaroo steak."

"There are *kangaroos* on this planet?"

"Well, not real kangaroo like back on Earth. In the first place these are only about a foot tall. But they're fat and juicy. How do you like it?"

Mark sank his teeth into a bite of the steak, and his eyes flew open with surprise. "Hey, this is great!"

"Hope you enjoy it. They can jump fifty feet in the air, so they're hard enough to catch."

"Well, I think it's worth it. And what is this?"

"Oh, that's tannberry juice. The berries only grow up in the mountains here. If you could synthesize it, you could make a fortune."

Mark tasted the juice and once again was pleasurably surprised. "This is better than Kool-Aid," he said.

"What's that?"

"Aw, it's a drink they used to have back on Earth to keep the kids quiet. Just kidding. But this is great stuff."

The two talked for a long time, reliving old memories. And then Zeigler said, "Come on, I want to show you some of the city."

They wandered through Memphis and finally, as Mark suspected would happen, wound up at a sort of tavern.

Inside, the place reminded Mark of any one of the thousand run-down bars that operated in this part of the galaxy. The air was smoke-filled. The lighting was dim. The smell of last month's spilled drinks was sour in his nostrils. He thought, *No matter where I go, there's always a place like this.*

Duke talked to the barkeeper and turned back to Edge. "Over there." He pointed with his index finger.

Finally they were sitting back in a dark corner, their voices low. Duke's eyes moved from person to person and were always watching the door.

"You act like you're going to get caught."

"Well, it doesn't hurt to be careful." The man grinned at him. His blond hair fell down over his eyes, and he brushed at it, saying, "So what are you doing here?"

"Oh, just a vacation."

Duke Zeigler studied his friend and then shook his head. "Don't give me that, Mark! I know that look. You're up to something."

"I never could fool you, could I?" Mark sipped his soda, then he leaned forward and said, "Tell me everything you know about the royal family."

"Oh, ho, so you're dealing that high on the deck! Well, since you ask, here's what I know." He took a long slow drink from his mug. "The king is named Denethor. His wife, the queen, is Teman, and the prince is named Arnon. For longer than anyone can remember, Denethor's ancestors have ruled Morlandria."

Duke paused to signal the waiter to bring him another round. "A long, long time ago, the Morlandria people discovered the ruins of an old shrine deep in the jungle. In fact, it's rumored to be not too far from Memphis. You know what I mean."

Edge spoke calmly. "No, I don't know what you mean."

"Originally the shrine was not built for Memphis but Memphis for the shrine. I believe they called it the 'Shrine of Ugarit.' Something like that." Already Duke appeared to be feeling the effects of the ale he had been drinking. "Anyway—" he put a hand on Edge's shoulder "—down through the years, the royal family was responsible for sacrificing thousands and thousands of people to some goddess. People will believe anything, you know that, Mark?"

"They sure will." Edge wanted Duke to keep talking, in the hope that maybe he would say something that would help him.

Duke seemed happy to go on. "Things stayed about the same around here until twelve or thirteen years ago."

"What happened?"

"Not a big thing, really, but it had big results." Duke winked at a dark-haired waitress who walked by. "A ship landed at the Memphis space port. Just a regular transport—nothing special about it. A man gets out of the ship and heads right to the palace. Now get this —it's the middle of the day, and all the guards have fallen asleep at their posts. The guy marches right into King Denethor's quarters without even so much as a by-your-leave."

"Why? Who was he?"

"And that's another thing! Nobody ever knew the man's name!"

"Well, what happened?"

"Now we're gettin' close to the good part. The man said he was a *Christian*. Nothing special, mind you, just a Christian. He told King Denethor and Queen Teman that this goddess they'd been worshiping was nothing but a lousy demon. The king, well, he was furious. He summoned the high priestess and ordered her to take the man and offer him to Astarte as a sacrifice."

"You seem to know a lot more about the royal family than you first let on." Edge was becoming engrossed in the tale.

"I'm not telling you anything that any five-year-old on this planet doesn't know." Duke finished his drink and waved at the waitress. "We're getting closer to that good part. They take the Christian to a cave located deep under the shrine. It's the same place where they'd offered sacrifices for untold years."

Duke watched the waitress place fresh ale and soda on the table, then turned back to Mark. "Now here's the good part. The story goes that this Astarte goddess *appeared*—right over the stone altar where they had the man tied down. Usually the person being sacrificed is screaming for their miserable life—but not this guy. He tells this apparition that he is saved by the blood of the Lamb, and he commands her to leave Morlandria. And off she goes, just like that."

"So then what happened. Did the king kill him or what?"

"When Astarte took off, everybody left the cave like madmen, except for the king and queen. They untied the man and told him that they'd never seen a god who could do something like that. This Astarte babe had terrorized Morlandria for years, and now she was gone in a few seconds. Well, Denethor and Teman became Christians themselves. They had Christian symbols and words engraved on top of the pictures of the goddess in the shrine, and then the king banned anyone from going into the shrine ever again. Morlandria was in a state of shock, I tell you."

"You mentioned a high priestess. What happened to her?"

"That was Zaria. Her father was King Denethor's cousin. He's dead now, and that leaves Zaria third in line for the throne. If something was to happen to King Denethor *and* Prince Arnon, Zaria would be the ruler of Morlandria."

"Did Zaria become a Christian, too?"

Duke laughed loud and long. "Zaria? A Christian! That's funny. Naw, she's worked real hard to reestablish Astarte worship. Right now, she has her hooks set real tight on Prince Arnon. I can understand his problem, though. She has a *power* of some kind. They say that when a man looks into her eyes, he loses all his willpower. I've heard that men have even killed for her. She's quite a lady." Duke downed the final dregs of his ale.

When his friend finally stopped talking, Edge sat quietly. He was trying to put together all of the instructions that he had received from Commandant Winona Lee. But at the same time he was trying to think how he could use Duke Zeigler. He was well aware that you can't stop an assassin with a feather duster, and the man across from him was just the one he would like to have on his side if trouble came.

Leaning forward, he grinned and said, "Duke, it's going to be like old times . . ."

6

Dangerous Souvenir

Jerusha was flanked by Raina and Ringo as they roamed from shop to shop. They were all acting silly, the result of long strain from the hard and perilous missions on other worlds. Now that there was no danger and there were no problems, they let themselves go.

Laughing, Raina said, "This is just like Disney World!"

"What's that?" Ringo asked, a puzzled frown on his face. "Seems I've heard of it somewhere."

"Oh, it was something Mei-Lani was telling me about. Back on Earth a long time ago, they had this wonderful park for kids to go to. It had people dressed in costumes. They were called names like Mickey Mouse and Donald Duck. And the place had all kinds of thrilling rides. It was a big thing back then."

Looking around her, Jerusha smiled. "Well, this isn't exactly like any of the films I've seen of Disney World, but it's sure better than some of the places we've been."

They wandered in and out of shops, buying small souvenirs and trinkets but mostly just looking. Underneath her light talk and laughter, however, Jerusha was aware that something seemed to be *wrong* with this city. She was extremely sensitive to things like that. She certainly could not read minds, and yet her friends were always amazed at the way it appeared she could. She was sensitive also to the emotions of others. Many

61

times she could sense raw anger beneath a smiling face.

"Do you feel anything special about this place? Either of you?"

"Not me," Ringo said, looking at her with surprise. He was holding up a small stuffed animal that looked like a cross between a squirrel and a tiger. It had long sharp teeth. He looked back at the object in his hand and said, "Now, this could take a plug out of you."

"What do you mean, 'special'?" Raina said. Her eyes were fixed on Jerusha.

Jerusha knew that Raina also was unusually sensitive. Perhaps Raina herself had been feeling something she could not identify. Something that made her very uncomfortable.

"I don't know, Raina." Jerusha hesitated. "It just feels sort of evil to me."

Ringo glanced around the shop. "I don't feel anything evil! I think this is a pretty nice store."

Raina shook her head. "No, Ringo, I think Jerusha is right. There's something wrong with more than this shop. I don't know what it is, but it's there."

As they went on to visit other stores and street displays, gradually both girls grew quieter, but Ringo appeared to be unconscious of the fears of his two friends. Finally they entered a store that had no windows at all. It was lighted by small lamps that glowed with a peculiar greenish tint.

"This is like being underwater," Jerusha muttered. "I don't care for this place much."

Ringo, however, did. He walked around, excited to find things that he was interested in. Finally he went off by himself into an even darker part of the store.

Raina and Jerusha looked for something to take

back to the ship. Then their eyes met, and Raina said, "This place is bad, Jerusha. Let's get out of here."

"I think you're right." Jerusha nodded and called, "Come on, Ringo!"

"What's he doing back there?" Raina asked.

"Oh, he's buying something. He's got his pockets stuffed full of junk."

A small statue caught Ringo's eye. It was standing on a shelf, alone.

Why, it's a statue of Sheva! he thought, excited. He glanced back at Raina. *I've heard about the love charms people used a long time ago. Maybe just having this would give me a better shot at making Raina like me.* Quickly he scooped up the statue. It felt strangely warm in his hands. "Boy, there's something to this thing!" he muttered. He went over to the counter to pay for it.

The shop owner, a tall, dark man whose eyes glittered, took the Intergalactic currency without a word. He did look oddly at Ringo, though, and then said, "You will find power in that, young man."

"Just what I need," Ringo replied. He went back to the girls.

Raina said, "What did you buy?"

"Oh, just this." Somehow Ringo felt uncomfortable showing the small object to the girls, but he did.

Both leaned forward in the murky light, and at once Jerusha shook her head. "I don't think this is a good thing for you to have. I wouldn't buy it if I were you, Ringo."

"It's just a keepsake!" Ringo said defensively. He shoved it into his pocket as the three of them left the store.

"I'm just going to give it to Jaleel as a gift," he said

when the girls continued to protest that he didn't need such a thing. But he was thinking, *They don't know everything, and there is some kind of power in this statue. I can just feel it!*

As the Space Rangers left the store, the owner leaned back against the wall. A small smile pulled up the corners of his thin lips, and he murmured, "So you want Sheva. Well, we will see how that works out!"

Heck, Dai, and Ivan had done their share of buying trinkets and were not interested in further shopping. But neither were they ready to go back to the *Daystar*. They kept on wandering the streets of Memphis until finally Ivan said, "What's that over there?"

"It looks like an amusement park to me," Heck said. "Come on! Let's see what's there!"

The section of the city that they had found was, indeed, an amusement park. There were rides, and things of little value for sale, and strange foods having little taste. They walked around, however, and looked at it all.

At one booth a tall, strong-looking man was advertised as Borsk, the Most Terrible Fighter in Memphis.

"Hmm," Ivan said. "They offer five hundred dinos to anybody that can stay with him for sixty seconds without getting knocked down. I think I'll have a go at him."

Ivan did, indeed, have a go and lasted no longer than thirty seconds. The big man from Memphis simply was too much for even Ivan's strength.

His two friends dragged him out of the ring, and when he woke up, he muttered, "What hit me?"

"I guess you better not try that again," Heck said.

Ivan's eye was almost closed. "I don't think I will. He's as tough as any I've seen."

Dai grinned. "I think *I'll* have a bout with him."

"Don't do it!" Heck said. "He could kill a fellow!"

Nevertheless, Dai walked up to the manager and said, "I'd like to go for a bout with your man."

The manager stared at him. "Young fellow, you don't want to commit suicide." But when Dai kept insisting, he said, "You understand the management takes no responsibility for injuries."

"That's all right," Dai said. He bounded up into the ring.

The manager went outside at once to announce the bout, and soon the place was filled with spectators.

Dai stood in a corner with Heck and Ivan as his seconds.

Heck looked across at the enormous fighter and said, "If he gets his hands on you, he'll kill you, Dai."

Then a gentle gong broke the silence, and cries went up from the crowd.

Dai stepped into the center of the ring.

The mighty Borsk came at him, his enormous hands outstretched. "I will feed you to the buzzards! You're a rash young fellow and need a lesson!" He made a quick lunge, but he might as well have lunged at air.

Dai, whose responses were almost superhuman, simply moved a few inches so that Borsk went crashing across the ring into the ropes.

The man spun around, his face purple with anger. "Oh, you're a dancer! We'll see about that!" As he came closer, his foot suddenly lashed out in a kick that would have probably killed Dai if it had landed.

Dai simply watched it come at him. Then he stepped to one side, and as the foot was even with his belt, he put a hand under the man's heel and lifted it.

Borsk fell to the canvas with a tremendous crash like a tree falling, and the crowd roared.

The manager shouted, "Get up, Borsk! You're going to lose all our money!"

But it was not even a contest! The huge man, who looked strong enough to pick up the building, could never lay a hand on the dark-haired young Ranger. Finally Borsk was gasping from exhaustion. Dai let him make one final lunge, then grabbed him by the wrist, and with a complicated maneuver sent him spinning through the air, carried by the force of his own momentum. He crashed into a post holding the ropes and, with a groan, simply lay still.

The manager shouted, "Foul! Foul!"

But Heck was a great manager for the moment. He shouted to the crowd, "He's trying to get out of paying the money! I think he's a crook!"

Before long, Dai, Heck, and Ivan were on the street outside the building. Dai was carrying his five hundred dinos.

"As your manager, I get ten percent of that, remember!" Heck told him.

"We'll divide it evenly," Dai said, and he gave a third of the coins to each of his friends. "Now, what will we do?" His eyes gleamed with fun. He was not even breathing hard.

"Well, what's that over there?" Heck asked, caressing his money before sticking it into his pocket.

"It says it's a fun house, whatever that is." Ivan frowned.

They stood staring at the outside advertising, making guesses as to what a fun house would be like.

Finally Heck said, "Well, let's go take a look. I could use a little fun."

They bought tickets and started down the fun

house passageways. Heck was in the lead, Ivan was next, and Dai was last in line.

First, they felt a jet of air blow against their legs.

"This is really scary," Heck said sarcastically.

"It's supposed to be a *fun* house, Ensign, not a haunted house," Ivan said. "This might be scary for a six-year-old, but someone your size, Heck, shouldn't be scared at all."

Heck laughed. "Maybe it's more scary because I'm so much higher in the atmosphere than you." At four feet six inches, Ivan was more than a foot shorter than Heck's five feet ten.

"I believe I have a way of bringing you down a couple of notches," Ivan said. "Not that I condone violence, but . . ."

Just as Heck walked past a chute that looked like a downhill slide, Ivan tackled him.

Both slid down the chute.

Dai ran to the slide. Then he heard the thump of bodies hitting the bottom. Suddenly there were screams.

Without hesitating, Dai jumped into the chute, shot down the slide, and within seconds found himself lying on his back beside Heck. Ivan was already on his feet and peering about in the semidarkness.

Dai could barely see the other two. "Is that you, Heck? Where are we?"

Heck's overweight body was not used to hitting the ground that hard. "I think I broke something."

Dai leaned closer to him. Heck was rubbing his hip, and Dai checked him for injuries. "I think the only thing that is injured is your pride."

"If you had even half the pride that I do, you'd understand why I'm so concerned about myself. I treat me like royalty!"

Dai rolled onto his feet, laughing.

"Careful," Ivan cautioned him. "Be careful. The ceiling is very low in here. We're in a tunnel, and it looks like the only way out is straight ahead."

As Dai's eyes grew accustomed to the dimness, he looked about the small area where they had landed. "This doesn't seem to be a fun house down here. If I were six years old, this place would be pretty scary."

Ivan was scratching his chin. "Looks like this tunnel goes deeper underground. I believe I see a faint light farther ahead, though."

"Come on, guys," Heck said nervously. "Let's look for another way out of here. I don't want to walk down any dark tunnel. What if something's in here!" Heck sounded really worried.

Dai turned to the slide they'd hurtled down. "We certainly can't climb this. It's too steep, and it's too slick," he said as he rubbed the slide's surface. "That leaves only one outlet—the tunnel. Whether we like it or not."

Ivan peered into the blackness. "I don't see a thing to give us trouble, Heck. There's just that faint light way down there, and that's good."

"You wouldn't be able to see spiders or bats on the walls! What if there's spiders and bats?"

Dai put his hand on Heck's arm. "I'll go first, then Ivan, then you. If anything happens, it will happen to us first."

"Aw, I'm sorry, Dai." Heck's voice was suddenly soft. He sounded much different from his usual boasting self. "I was trapped in a cave one time, and there were spiders and bats in there. Do you know what it's like to be standing alone in the dark with hundreds of bats flying around your head?"

"No, I don't."

"It might not be scary to you, but it terrified me.

And I couldn't crouch down because of the spiders on the ground. They were as big across as my hand, with huge luminous eyes. Sometimes I still have nightmares about them."

Ivan interjected, "Heck, I promise you'll be all right. Usually I can *smell* bats if they're around, and also I don't see any luminous eyes moving around in there."

"OK, Ivan. I trust you and Dai. But if it were just me, I'd die right here before I'd walk into that tunnel."

Dai started cautiously down the passage, keeping his eyes on the glow far ahead. Although he felt no cobwebs against his face, he did run into an occasional tree root hanging from the ceiling. He tried to hold the roots out of Heck's way—Ivan was too short for them to be a problem for him. But one apparently brushed across the top of Heck's head.

"Yow!" Heck screamed in terror, charged past Ivan, and almost made it past Dai. But Dai's grip on his arm was like iron, and Heck hit the ground screaming.

Ivan said angrily. "Will you shut up! It was just a tree root. Now everyone in the place will know we're here."

"You said nothing was here!"

Dai glanced toward the light down the tunnel. It was growing brighter, he thought. In fact, he could now see that it was orange and red and appeared to be swirling around.

"Looks to me like that could be some sort of gas," Dai said as he helped Heck to his feet.

Ivan had crept a few feet farther along. Suddenly he said, "Both of you come here. I think I've found something. There's a small patch of light shining on the floor."

"So what? You've found a tiny light on the floor. How does that help us?" Sarcasm was back in Heck's voice, betraying him. Dai had discovered that using sarcasm was the way Heck tried to cover up his weaknesses.

As Dai and Heck came to Ivan's side, the chief engineer said, "Ensign, don't look down—look *up*. The light is shining down on us."

Both Dai and Heck looked upward, and Dai said, "Praise the Lord!"

There was an air shaft leading to the surface.

But the orange and red glow down the tunnel was turning more angry-looking by the second. The swirling light looked like an inferno now. Suddenly there was a blast of sound, and the flaming caldron was moving toward them.

"Got to make it to the surface fast, or we'll be fried for sure!" Ivan jumped upward but was unable to reach the shaft.

Quickly Dai lifted the dwarf and placed him in the air passage. There were plenty of uneven places in the rock sides to provide handholds.

Heck looked at Dai and shook his head. "I can't jump up either. I'm too heavy. You go on without me, Dai. Quick. Save yourself!"

"Heck, that's the most noble thing I've ever heard you say. There's hope for you yet!"

The next instant, Heck was flying straight up into the air shaft, where Ivan grabbed his hand, yelling, "Now, climb! Follow me!"

The three shipmates scrambled frantically upward and one by one threw themselves out onto the surface. Just as Dai Bando cleared the shaft, a column of superhot gas shot skyward.

Ivan was breathing heavily. He managed to say, "One more second in there, and we would all be dead."

Heck was regaining his breath. "I know I was

being sarcastic a while ago—but I was scared stiff. I can't imagine being more scared."

Dai, who had practically carried Heck up the shaft on his shoulders, wondered aloud, "But why would a fun house have something so dangerous located in it? Children could be burned alive in there. It was only by the grace of God that we were saved!"

Ivan got to his feet next to him. "Maybe that was the whole point. Maybe something evil is located at the end of that tunnel. Something that didn't like us. Something that didn't want us coming down." Ivan folded his arms and walked a few steps away. Then he turned back and said, "Heck, I have a weakness, too."

"What is that?" Heck asked, his eyes still squinting from the sunlight.

"I'm afraid of being burned alive."

Dai decided it was time to make their way back to the *Daystar*. "We were all pretty shaken up. My Aunt Bronwen once said that 'something evil this way comes.' We should be on guard. This planet isn't as beautiful as it looks!"

7

Prince Arnon

The afternoon sun was beginning to set over the city of Memphis as Mark Edge and Temple Cole walked up to the gates of the palace.

Leaning back and straining his neck, Edge surveyed the tall building. It was constructed of pink marble and set with towers and pointed spires. "Quite a little shack, isn't it, Temple?"

"I suppose it's the most imposing structure in Memphis." She admired its smooth, rounded turrets but then looked toward the palace entrance and frowned. "I just wish we knew more about the royal family we're about to visit."

"Well, I found out one thing. The king and the queen are both *Christians.*"

"Is that right? How did you find that out?"

"Oh, you know how Mei-Lani is. She's quite a historian and seems to have her finger in every pie. She found out about it somehow."

He did not tell her that he had also gotten considerable information from Duke Zeigler. Mark and his old friend had talked for hours during their evening together, and the captain believed he now had some inside information that would prove quite helpful. "Well, come along, Dr. Cole. Let's meet the royal family."

They were halted at the gate by two tall guards, who questioned them.

But when the guards discovered their identity, one of them nodded. "Yes, indeed. The king is expecting you." He lifted a hand, and a short young man in a scarlet uniform approached at once. "Take these two up to the king. They are expected."

"Of course. If you will come this way . . ."

Mark and Temple were soon lost in the maze of corridors through which the official led them.

"How many rooms are there in this palace?" Temple asked cautiously.

"Over five hundred, I believe."

"It would make a good motel!"

"What is a motel?"

"A place on Earth where people pay to stay the night. You could make a lot of money that way!" She smiled.

"I'm sure that would not interest His Majesty." Stopping at last before a door, their guide said, "It is Morlandria protocol for visitors to honor Their Majesties by crawling in on their hands and knees."

"I think we'll omit that," Edge said firmly. He turned to Temple. "I don't feel much like crawling, do you?"

"No, I think a simple bow will do for both of us."

The man shrugged. "Be it on your own heads." He opened the door wide.

Mark and Temple stepped into what struck the captain as a rather simple room for royalty. It was no more than twenty feet wide and thirty feet long and was obviously a chamber where the royal family met their guests. The furniture consisted of a table made of dark wood and a dozen chairs around it, all upholstered in rich maroon. The walls were ornamented with pictures of what Edge assumed to be ancestors of the present royal family.

"Welcome to Memphis." The king was an extremely tall man with white hair and a clipped beard. His sharp blue eyes were highly intelligent, and on the whole his face gave the impression of strength. "I am King Denethor, and this is Queen Teman."

Both Edge and Dr. Cole bowed deeply, and then the captain said, "We are happy to be on your planet, Your Majesty. I am Captain Mark Edge, and this is Dr. Temple Cole, our flight surgeon."

"You must have had a long journey," Queen Teman said. "Let me offer you refreshments."

Soon the four were seated about the table, and Temple was, for the most part, listening without saying much. She thought Queen Teman an attractive woman. The queen was somewhere in her late forties, she judged, and of average height. She had blonde hair, dark blue eyes, and there was a gentleness in her face that drew Temple immediately.

As the men talked of the politics of the Intergalactic Council, she found herself speaking of other things, more womanly things, with the queen. Soon she discovered that the queen's heart was filled with hope for her son, Prince Arnon. Queen Teman's face glowed as she described him.

"You're very proud of your son, Your Majesty," Temple said with a smile.

And then a troubled light flickered in the queen's eyes. She bowed her head for a moment, and her lips tightened.

Instantly Temple perceived that there was a problem here.

The king had overheard that part of their conversation, and he reached over to take his wife's hand. "We *have* been proud of our son—but recently there has been difficulty. He is twenty-five now and the heir to my throne, of course, and I had planned to step down very soon . . ."

When the king broke off, Edge asked quietly, "What sort of problem are you having, Your Highness— or is it too personal?"

"It is both personal and political, and I'm afraid it's no secret." He shook his head sadly, and his face wore a troubled expression. "The queen and I quite recently became Christians, and we're very happy to have the Lord Jesus in our lives, but—"

The queen broke in. "Our son has become . . . involved . . . with a woman of whom we are quite disapproving."

The captain's glance met Temple's, and she saw that both of them were thinking the same thing.

"I'm sorry to hear that," Mark said. "It seems many young men have that trouble." He frowned. "I did myself."

"No, it is not what you think," King Denethor said instantly. "The woman I speak of is Zaria, the high priestess of Astarte, a very beautiful woman. The problem is that our son has not only fallen in love with her, but she has enticed him into the worship of the goddess."

"It's caused us much grief, as you may imagine," the queen said quietly.

Temple Cole saw the pain in the woman's eyes, and it was reflected in the eyes of the king. Quietly she said, "I'm not a parent, but—from what I've seen and heard from parents—I gather that the greatest pain of all comes from children."

"I think that is right," the king agreed, "and in this case there seems to be nothing that we can do about it except pray."

"Why is this also political, Your Majesty?" Edge questioned. "It seems to be a private matter."

"No, it is not. You see, I come from a very small

76

family. Zaria's father, who died last year, was a distant cousin of mine. As always in matters like this, it is complicated. If I died, and if Arnon also died, Zaria would be the ruler of the planet."

"Oh, I see! That does make things different, doesn't it?"

"Yes, it does." King Denethor's expression now became grim. "And even if Arnon did survive me and assume the throne . . . well, this woman has something about her that I cannot explain."

"*I* can explain, I think," Queen Teman said confidently. "She has dark powers. As a matter of fact, those who worship Astarte often call her the Queen of Darkness. Her high priestess is a very powerful woman, Captain Edge. Not only does she control a considerable part of the population—those who have fallen into the worship of this terrible goddess—but she seems to have power even to cloud the minds of people."

"That is correct, and it is a rather frightening thing," King Denethor said. "I believe our son has fallen completely under her influence."

And then the door abruptly burst open.

The young man who came in was easily recognizable. *That's Prince Arnon*, Temple said to herself. *He looks exactly like a younger edition of his father.*

Arnon was a tall youth and handsome, having the fair coloring of his mother and the strength of his father. Now, however, his face was flushed with anger, and he brushed aside the introductions to the guests offered by his father.

"I've come to talk to you about Zaria!"

"Son, this is not the time for that."

"It *is* the time, for I will make it so!" Arnon began to shout demands at his parents, who were obviously holding in their tempers. Prince Arnon concluded his tirade by yelling, "You will find it hard to control Zaria as you have controlled me!"

"We have never attempted to control you, my son," Denethor said gently.

"You have! You tried to force me to become a Christian! I'll have none of it, do you hear!" Fury turned his handsome face ugly, and he stormed from the room, slamming the door behind him.

"You see how he is now, but you should have known him before he met Zaria," Queen Teman said softly. "He was the most gentle, the most courteous young man I had ever seen."

"There's a darkness that's clouded him," King Denethor said. "*Her* darkness. And I see no good end to this business."

Zaria, high priestess of Astarte, was half reclining on a couch covered with a soft, silky material. She was a tall woman with jet black hair and eyes fully as dark. She was wearing a black gown.

The priestess looked up at the servant who had come in with a question, and she nodded. "Allow Prince Arnon to enter."

"Yes, my queen."

As she waited for the prince to arrive, a smile touched Zaria's lips. "So. I have drawn him back. He is a foolish young man, which is good." She rose as Arnon came in, however, and welcomed him with a kiss. "Prince," she said. "I have missed you. Come. Sit down. Let me give you something to drink."

Arnon's face still retained some of his anger, for he had come directly from his parents. But he sat down and soon was drinking from a golden goblet. He never knew what the drink was, for Zaria had laughingly said, "This is my secret formula. A love potion."

Then she sat down beside him. "You're troubled. I can always tell. What's the matter, my prince?"

"It's my parents! They won't listen to me! This foolish Christianity they've fallen into—it's changed them completely!"

"Yes, I've found that always to be the case. It is a foolish religion. The idea that a man dying thousands of years ago could help anybody today is ridiculous!"

"That's what I keep telling them!"

Zaria well knew that Arnon did not realize how deeply he was in the grip of her dark powers. He had merely parroted to his parents that which she had put into his mind. "Your father and mother are deceived. As a good son, it is up to you to see that they come to their senses."

"How can I do that? They are so convinced that Jesus Christ is God. There is nothing I can do."

"Yes, there is something you can do, but it will be very hard."

Quickly Arnon looked up. "And what is that?"

"I will tell you later. Drink now, and I will cause your anger to pass away." She smiled at him archly and touched the cup, lifting it to his lips.

He was no doubt wondering what she could mean about his parents, she thought. But the room was full of rich incense, and his mind would soon be swimming.

Zaria continued to smile. At the same time, she was thinking, *You foolish boy! Just give me a little time, and you will kill your parents. Then you will be king. But not for long.*

Her mind raced ahead, and with no regret at all she created a plan for ridding herself of Arnon. *Then,* she thought triumphantly, *I will be queen of the planet with no one to challenge me. This Jesus cannot stand against me!*

79

8

The Shrine in the Jungle

Jerusha looked around the teenager nightclub and sniffed. "It doesn't look like a place *I* would enjoy much."

"Oh, come on! It'll be fun!" Ringo said.

It had been Ringo who had seen the advertising for the club. He loved loud music, and he figured that this place would provide it. Once again he fingered the image of Sheva in his pocket and thought about how it was going to help him with Raina. He didn't know exactly how it would work, but he would talk to Tara Jaleel. She would know.

A small band, consisting of some familiar instruments and some that Jerusha did not know, was blasting away with full power. A little woman with purple hair and a green jumpsuit seemed about to swallow the microphone as she gargled unrecognizable words into it.

"If that's singing, I don't recognize it," Raina St. Clair said.

The large room was filled with dancing teenagers. Colored lights flickered overhead, throwing their glow over the faces of the young people. And beneath the sound of the blaring music there was the babble of laughter and loud talk.

"Let's just go," Jerusha said. "I don't care for this."

She half turned and then abruptly stopped, for a couple had planted themselves directly in front of her.

"Why, hello, Jerusha!" Karl Bentlow's handsome face reflected the orange and green lights shining down from the ceiling. He was wearing a light green uniform that showed off his tall athletic figure well, and he was smiling with anticipation. "I didn't expect to see *you* here," he said. "How about a dance?"

"Oh, I don't think so, Karl," Jerusha said quickly. "We're leaving."

"Oh, come on. Just one, and then we'll see where it goes."

Jerusha suddenly found herself being led out onto the dance floor. She gave a despairing look back at Raina, then Jerusha said, "No, Karl. Let's just talk."

"Well, what are you three doing here?" Olga asked. A displeased expression darkened her face as her eyes followed Jerusha and Karl. She too was wearing a light green uniform, and her brown hair was clipped shorter than ever. She finally gave Ringo and Raina her full attention. "What are you doing on Morlandria?"

Before Ringo could speak, Raina said, "You'll have to ask Captain Edge that."

None of the Space Rangers had much liking for Olga Von Kemp. When they had been students together at the Intergalactic Academy, Olga had done all she could to ridicule those who were Christians. Raina, Ringo remembered, had come in for a great deal of Olga's verbal abuse.

Now Raina reversed the girl's question. "What are you and Karl doing on Morlandria?"

"You know it's against the policy for Intergalactic officers to tell anything about their missions. You didn't forget *everything* when you got kicked out, did you, Raina?"

Raina St. Clair lowered her head.

Ringo saw that the reminder that she had been expelled from the Space Academy was still painful for Raina to bear, and he decided to pick up the conversation. "Come on, Olga. Let's get something to eat."

He did not like the girl any more than the other Space Rangers did, but he'd seen that she was hurting Raina, and he was determined to put a stop to it. Seizing her arm, he dragged Olga toward the refreshment table.

As they helped themselves, he looked across to where Jerusha and Karl were standing. "They make a good-looking couple, don't they?" he asked. Then he grinned, knowing that Olga was fiercely jealous over Karl Bentlow.

"She always did throw herself at Karl!"

"I thought it was the other way around."

Across the noisy room, Karl was telling Jerusha loudly and at length about the Convette. "Too bad you have to dash around space in an old bucket like the *Daystar.*"

"I wouldn't call the *Daystar* an old bucket. She may not be a brand-new Convette, but Captain Edge gets all that can be gotten out of a ship. He's a fine captain."

"Doesn't it make you feel bad, Jerusha?"

"Doesn't what make me feel bad?"

The music was harsh and grating, and Jerusha tried to focus on the conversation.

"Why, I mean you've really come down in the world. You were the prize student there at the Academy, and now you're reduced to flying around with a bunch of rejects and with a captain that's little better than a pirate."

"He's not a pirate!"

Karl Bentlow stared at her. "You're very defensive, Ensign Ericson. You're not falling for this guy, are you?"

"Of course not!"

"Well, I wouldn't think so! He's an old man!"

"He's not twenty-five years old!"

"Well, you're only fifteen, so that settles that!"

Unhappy with these remarks, Jerusha tried to change the subject. "Let me ask *you* a question. Are you happy serving under a woman like Commander Inch?" And she saw Karl's face flush.

"Commander Inch is all right."

"She's mean as a snake, and you know it."

"That's because you didn't get along with her. I found out how to wind her around my little finger." He smiled, and a dimple appeared in each cheek.

Jerusha found herself wondering what exactly was going on. "This is a strange part of the galaxy for her to send you with that Convette," she ventured.

"Well, Commander Inch has big things in mind."

"What sort of things?"

Karl's eyes began to glow with excitement. "Commander Inch has entrusted Olga and me with a special mission. We're to make contact here on Morlandria with a woman by the name of Zaria. She's the high priestess of Astarte and third in line for the throne. She's really an important person on this planet, and Commander Inch wants to meet her. So we'll arrange it."

"I don't think you're on a very safe mission. You'd better be careful, Karl."

"Don't worry about us. We'll be all right. Now, how about if you and I go out and see some more spots, Jerusha?"

"No, I've got to get back to the ship."

84

It was obvious that Karl was not accustomed to having young women turn down his invitations. He flushed and said, "See you around, Jerusha. Don't get that jalopy in front of our ship. We might run over it." He crossed the floor to rejoin Olga, who looked toward Jerusha with triumph as he led her out among the dancers.

Finding her two friends, Jerusha said grimly, "Let's get out of here."

Ringo grinned. "Did you get enough of Karl?"

"Yes, plenty."

"Well, I'm ready if you are."

"So am I," Raina said.

Ringo seemed so happy that Jerusha whispered, "What's he so happy about, Raina?"

"I don't know. But he's got something on his mind that's making him feel better. I'd like to know what it is."

"So would I."

The trip to the shrine took a long time, for it was some distance from the city. The Land Rover was very powerful and was able to maneuver in the worst terrain, but the ride was hard and jolting. The "Bone-Crusher" shook Mei-Lani, Bronwen, and Thrax severely, for the roads were deeply rutted.

"This would shake my brains out if I had any," Thrax muttered. He gripped the wheel and clenched his teeth. "It's harder to drive this thing than it was to fly the old *Daystar.*"

Bronwen said nothing. She was concerned with holding on.

Then Thrax looked down at the map and took a right turn into the jungle. He said, "I think it's about a quarter of a mile down this way."

"Can't be too soon for me," Mei-Lani said. "I didn't

know the roads would be so rough." She looked up at the towering trees that darkened the sky, but then suddenly they were driving in a more open space, and she cried out with delight, "There it is!"

Thrax pulled the vehicle to a stop, and Bronwen and Mei-Lani gratefully got out.

They all stood staring in silence at the old shrine. It rose into the sky, a white structure, now vine-covered, and built of what seemed to be pure alabaster. An arched open gateway invited entrance.

Then Zeno Thrax said, "Let me make a quick reconnaissance to make sure there's nothing dangerous around here."

As soon as he disappeared, Mei-Lani looked at Bronwen Llewellen and said, "Bronwen, do you think . . ."

Bronwen turned to look at the girl, of whom she was very fond. "What is it, Mei-Lani?" With her gift of discernment, she perceived that the girl was deeply troubled. She moved closer and put her arm around Mei-Lani's shoulder. "You've been trying to tell me something for some time now. Can't you do it?"

Mei-Lani seemed to struggle with the thoughts that arose in her. She moistened her lips and said, "I want to talk to somebody. I—"

But at that moment Thrax returned, looking satisfied. "It's all right! Nothing around to give us any problem!" Then he looked from Bronwen to Mei-Lani and halted abruptly. "I'm not interrupting something, am I?"

"No, no," Mei-Lani said.

Bronwen kept her eyes on the girl's face. *I'll have to get alone with her and let her take her time. Something's troubling her, and she can't talk about it.*

"Let's start exploring," the girl said quickly. She appeared embarrassed by the fact that she had almost spoken whatever was on her mind.

As they walked around inside the shrine, Mei-Lani told them its history. Bronwen was fascinated, and both she and Zeno began to ask questions. Oddly, more than once, while examining the strange engravings on the shrine walls, Bronwen thought she heard voices echoing. But that was impossible. Where would anyone be?

Then Mei-Lani pointed to the walls that adjoined the entrance. "Now *that's* strange! Some *Christian* engravings have been etched over the pictures of Astarte. See? And over there—" she pointed to another wall "—the face of Astarte has been scratched off the wall, and a cross has been drawn over it!"

Bronwen examined the mutilated artwork. "Some spiritual war has been waged in this place in time past. I can sense it."

Thrax sighed loudly. "For goodness' sake, does everything have to be 'spiritual'?"

Bronwen threw up her hands, saying, "Zeno, Zeno, haven't you seen enough yet with all the things we've been through?"

Mei-Lani interjected, "I remember what my parents said. Long ago this place was used for human sacrifices. I had not imagined that any evil would still be here. But, Bronwen, I feel it, too."

Thrax was starting to disagree when Bronwen got their attention by holding a finger to her lips. There were definitely voices, and they were becoming louder!

9
The Fun House

I don't care what you think now," Dai Bando said, "something happened in that fun house that I didn't like!"

He stood staring at Heck and Ivan defiantly. Now that they were back at the *Daystar*, the other two seemed to have lost their fear. The life-and-death experience in the tunnel appeared to be quickly fading from their minds.

Too quickly, Dai thought.

Their experience at the fun house had shaken Dai, though. He said, "I wish we hadn't even gone into that place."

"Me too!" Heck shrugged his shoulders. "I thought it was supposed to be fun."

Chief Engineer Ivan Petroski was a strange contrast to the two Rangers. He was thirty years old and was only four feet six inches tall. He was well proportioned, however, and on his home planet, Bellinka 2, all the people were to his scale. As a matter of fact, he was one of the taller members of the community.

He stroked his chin thoughtfully. "Well, what do you think it was, Dai?" he asked.

"There's something . . . something evil about that place."

Petroski raised his eyebrows. "You mean there was some kind of evil spirit in there? I don't believe in such things as that. I'm just not a superstitious man."

"Me either," Heck said. "I didn't feel any demons. Spiders and bats, maybe, but no demons!"

Dai well knew that Heck Jordan was not in the least inclined toward such matters. His ambition in life was just to get rich, wear expensive clothes, eat all that he could, and dazzle the girls.

Heck shifted uneasily from foot to foot, then said, "I'm afraid this Christianity is going to drive you crazy, Dai. You're starting to see a demon behind every bush."

This was not true, but Dai Bando did not bother to deny it. He knew that his two friends had no spiritual discernment.

Dai, however, had discovered that the closer he walked with God, the more sensitive he was to spiritual matters. And he had definitely felt *something* evil in that place.

"I'm not going back there!" he announced. He turned and walked into the port of the *Daystar*, leaving the other two staring after him.

"Dai's a nice fellow, but he's too superstitious," the chief engineer said. "That fun house was a strange place all right, and *maybe* somebody was trying to kill us for some reason"—Ivan was becoming more uncertain— "but I can't buy the supernatural stuff."

Actually, Ivan was convinced that there *had* been something sinister about the fun house, but he had his reputation to maintain. And, in all truth, he was secretly impressed by the young Rangers. He knew that all of them except Heck professed to be Christians, and, although he fought against it, Petroski also knew that they had something that was quite admirable.

Something dangerous *had* happened in the fun house. As Heck left him standing alone at the *Daystar* port, Petroski looked up at the dark skies and considered what had occurred.

Then he thought, *Well, if You're up there and You helped us somehow, thank You very much!*

Trying to shake off his sober mood, Ivan entered the cruiser.

In the rec room, Petroski found Tara Jaleel sitting at a table with Dai and Heck, who were having a discussion about something. Jaleel was leaning forward and listening carefully. Her face was smooth as ivory, and her large luminous eyes seemed to be devouring Dai as he described the incident at the fun house. Petroski was interested in her reaction.

"This whole planet is somehow wrong," Dai said. "I think it's because of idol worship of some kind."

"But what you call idol worship is not bad, Dai," Tara Jaleel said. She shrugged her muscular shoulders. "You've just got to learn that there are supernatural powers that can make things better for us. I know you're afraid of those things, Dai, but you're wrong."

Dai gazed at her, then shook his head. "No, I don't think so."

As soon as Dai left the rec room for his quarters, Petroski said, "He's a strange young fellow."

"Yes, he is. And he needs to be enlightened."

"So do it!" Heck said. "What's going on?"

"I think all of us need help," Tara Jaleel said.

This certainly surprised Petroski. "That's strange coming from you, Tara. You're very independent."

"None of us is truly independent," she said. "I get my strength from—" She broke off and appeared to think for a moment before saying, "I get my strength from other sources."

"That's what these Christians say, too," Petroski said. "You're not one of them, are you?"

"No, indeed. I follow Sheva."

For some reason just the name seemed to be ominous, and the chief engineer felt a chill go up his back. He got up from the table. "Well, *I'm* independent! I don't need anybody or anything!" He pushed in his chair and walked off as a disdainful smile formed on the lips of Tara Jaleel.

"This is some place, Olga."

"I've certainly never seen anything quite like it."

Karl Bentlow and Olga Von Kemp stood in the reception room of the high priestess of Astarte. They had been excited about their mission ever since leaving Earth but especially now. It seemed that things were beginning to happen.

Karl said as much, his eyes shining. "I'm anxious to meet this Zaria, the high priestess."

He did not have long to wait, for from somewhere a regal-looking woman came in. She was almost as tall as Karl himself, and she was very beautiful.

"I am Zaria, high priestess of Astarte, and you are Ensign Bentlow?" She put out her hand and gave him a seductive smile, then turned to nod slightly and stare at Olga. "And you are Ensign Von Kemp. Welcome to Morlandria."

Karl was stunned by the high priestess's exceptional beauty. He was also vaguely aware that some strange force seemed to emanate from her. He had never been in the presence of a woman exactly like this, and he found it hard to speak.

Zaria smiled. "Come. Sit down." She led them to a couch and a chair and said, "Sit beside me, Ensign Bentlow."

Olga Von Kemp, always jealous over Karl, frowned but silently took her seat across from the priestess. There Olga sat quietly, apparently trying to figure Zaria out.

Karl Bentlow then did a very unwise thing. He felt so ill at ease in the presence of the priestess that he began to boast. "We are Commander Inch's trusted officers, and she's given us the power to negotiate."

"I'm glad to hear that. You will give me her message."

Karl suddenly decided that what this woman needed was to see a strong man. He blustered, "I will give the orders here, Zaria! You may be priestess of whatever you choose, but we are representatives of the Intergalactic Council!"

This was not true, of course, but it seemed Karl could not help himself. He was determined to overpower this arrogant woman with his authority.

Olga's eyes flew open. "Karl," she began, "we'd better—"

"I'll handle this, Olga!" he snapped. He was slightly blinded by what was going on, so he did not pay attention to the expression on Zaria's face. He got to his feet, saying, "You'll have to come to our ship. We'll negotiate there!"

"No, you will not negotiate at all!"

"What did you say?" Karl asked rather stupidly. He noticed that the room seemed to be swimming in a haze, and as Zaria also stood, he felt himself growing weak all over.

"You will not negotiate at all, you poor fool!" she repeated. "You have a message from Commander Inch, and you will give it to me at once!"

Karl dimly remembered the instructions that Commander Inch had given him, but his mind was growing cloudier and cloudier.

"I see that you will do very well for my purposes," Zaria said coldly. "Give me the message!"

For some reason Karl could not move very well.

He sensed that something very unusual, even awe-some, was going on.

Swiftly, Olga crossed to him and pulled the small envelope out of a pocket in his tunic. She looked very frightened.

"Here it is," Olga said quickly. "We'd better go now."

"You're not going anywhere!"

They stared at Zaria.

"Astarte will have her sacrifices, and you two will do very well."

"No—no!" Olga cried.

She whirled and tried to escape. But then some force appeared to seize her, and she fell to the floor of the reception hall.

Karl too collapsed, and he knew no more.

Olga awoke after a period of time impossible to determine. She did not know where she was, but over-head were trees and exotic flowers. Then, hazily, she saw that two large men were carrying Karl into a white building.

They'll be back for me! she thought frantically. She struggled to her feet, and with one more distraught look toward the men and Karl, she began to stagger toward the jungle. She gained strength as she began to run.

Olga had no idea where she was going. She only knew that it was death to stay here. The girl had never prayed in her life, but now she did pray. She did not know to whom she prayed, and her prayer was a silent scream. *Oh, help me! They're going to kill me! Don't let me die!*

10

Double Cross

Nervously, Temple Cole sat down on the beige upholstered chair in Captain Edge's cabin. She was off duty and was wearing a plum colored tunic and an abbreviated skirt. Around her neck was a gold chain that suspended a deep violet stone that exactly matched her eyes.

Temple always felt somewhat strange being there, partly because she was drawn to this tall, broad-shouldered man in a way that disturbed her. She accepted the drink of juice that he offered her. "Thank you, Mark."

"You're welcome." Taking his own cup of scalding black coffee, Edge sat across from her and took a swallow.

He did not flinch, and Temple said with a smile, "You must have burned out all your taste buds. You can drink the hottest coffee of any person I've ever seen."

"Matter of practice," he said, returning her smile.

For a time they simply sat and listened to the soft music that filled the cabin. Finally the captain said, "We've come a long way, haven't we, Temple?"

For a moment she pretended that she did not understand his meaning. When Dr. Cole had come to the *Daystar* as a late member of the crew, almost at once she had sensed that Captain Edge was attracted to her. But despite the closeness that had developed during their adventures together, she still had strange feelings about the situation.

"What's the matter, Temple? You find me homely or boring?"

"Not at all, Mark!"

"You act like it sometimes. It's like you have a wire fence around yourself with a big sign that says, 'Keep out! No admittance!' It gets to a fellow after a while."

She took occasion to sip her juice in order to smother her feelings. The delay did not succeed, however, and she knew exactly why. Now she finally knew that she would have to tell Mark more.

"I suppose what you say is true. But when someone gets burned, she dreads the fire."

"We all get burned at one time or other. I've been scorched a good many times myself. But, Temple, you can't crawl into a hole and live small ever after."

She shook her head in disagreement. "It's not that simple for me. Maybe it's easier for a man than for a woman."

"What's easier?"

"Rejection. Betrayal."

"I know. You're talking about that captain of yours that pulled the plug on you!"

Temple's mouth turned into a firm line, and her eyes half closed as she thought of the most bitter incident in her life. She had been in love with the captain of a star cruiser. There had been a terrible accident, and most of the crew had been lost. Temple had looked to the captain for help, but, instead, he blamed the entire disaster on her, despite the fact that he had protested over and over that he loved her. The memory was still hard for her to bear.

The doctor got up and walked over to the port to look out at the stars floating in black space. "That's right," she said briefly.

"I don't think you're going to be happy until you're

able to put that behind you, Temple. You've got to find somebody to trust."

"I *did* trust someone, remember! And I got thrown to the wolves."

"But everybody's not like that captain."

She turned and studied his face. It was a strong face. His blue gray eyes were extremely alert. "You think I ought to trust *you?*"

"Sure."

"Mark, I know a little bit about your past. You haven't kept a very low profile."

Uncomfortably, he moved around on his seat. Then he put down his coffee and walked over to her. "I'll admit I haven't had a perfect record—"

"I'm afraid you were just a little short of being a pirate, Mark Edge. Anyone who works for Sir Richard Irons isn't anywhere close to perfection!"

As always when reminded that he had once worked for the most immoral—and in some ways the most powerful—man in the galaxy, Edge grew defensive. "Well, I don't work for him now! He's got black dirt on his hands, but it doesn't have to rub off on anybody!"

"I wasn't only speaking of that. You've had quite a few girlfriends in the past, haven't you?"

He flushed. "I've known a few girls."

"So your record isn't very good there, either. But you want me to trust you."

"Yes, I want you to trust me."

"I just can't do it right now, Mark."

Ultimately this conversation played itself out, and he threw up his hands. "All right, if you're going to be a hermit—or a hermitess—I can't stop you."

"I'm sorry, Mark. It truly isn't all you. It's me. I just haven't been able to get over my problems."

Sighing deeply, Edge said, "Well, maybe you will

before this is over. Anyhow, I think it's time to tell you about our mission."

"Mission? I thought we were ordered here just to get some rest and relaxation."

"That's what I told the crew, because that's what Commandant Lee ordered me to tell them. But that's not the way it is. We've come here to stop the king from being assassinated."

"Assassinated? How can that be?" Temple listened with astonishment as the captain related the essence of their orders.

"So we're supposed to protect the king. How can we do that? He's inside his palace! He has hundreds of guards already!"

"I think the guards are going to be looking for quite a different enemy. From what I hear from my friend Duke Zeigler, the king and queen are in danger from somebody a lot closer than they think."

Temple's eyes narrowed as she thought of their interview with the royal family. "You mean a relative, don't you? Prince Arnon?"

"His may be the hand to do it. But after what I saw today, I'd look at Zaria, the high priestess of Astarte."

Quickly Temple thought of Prince Arnon's flushed face and also how confused he had seemed. "You may be exactly right," she said.

"You know what they say—'Look for the woman.'"

"So a woman always has to be the villain! I'm not sure about that, but I do think you're right this time. Arnon could be very dangerous. What are you going to do about it?"

"Stop him somehow!"

If Edge had known what was happening in the palace at that moment, he would have been more concerned about the success of his mission. Prince Arnon, infatuated by Zaria, had agreed to capture his parents and to assume the throne. Leading a handpicked group of Zaria's men, he burst into the throne room.

"My son, what are you doing?" King Denethor cried out. He moved over to put his arm around his wife when he saw the armed men clothed in black and wearing the insignia of Astarte.

"Father, I've tried to talk sense to you, and you won't listen, and now I'm going to have to take stronger steps!"

"I see," Denethor said. "I see that you've found a quick way to seize the throne—by putting us out of the way."

"Just for a while, Father. And you'll be safe enough," Arnon said. His mind was still somewhat cloudy, but, even so, he could not meet the sad gaze of his mother, who stood saying nothing. "You'll be well cared for. I promise. You've been confused by this Christianity that you've accepted hook, line, and sinker! I am taking over in order to keep the planet from going completely in that direction!"

"This isn't you, my son. This is Zaria," the queen said.

Even in his confusion, Prince Arnon could feel himself flush. This time he managed to meet his mother's eyes. He saw no anger there but only sorrow. "I—I don't want to discuss it, Mother." He turned to the guards. "You will take them to the dungeon!"

"And take him as well!"

Prince Arnon whirled to see Zaria at the door.

The priestess smiled cruelly. "You fool, do you think I would trust a man who would betray his own parents? If you would betray them, you would betray me."

"Zaria, what are you talking about?" Arnon cried. He started toward her but suddenly felt as if he had run into a wall. He cried out.

The high priestess said, "Take him to the dungeon as well! Seize them all!"

"Zaria, you can't do this!"

"Can I not? When the torturer comes, we will have every state secret out of all of you! Take them away!"

Prince Arnon still could not believe what was happening. He stared at the beautiful priestess and said, "I thought—I thought you cared for me."

"I did care for you. You were the key to getting exactly what I wanted. Soon this planet will see a new ruler. They sometimes call me the Queen of Darkness. In the future they will call me that *and* Queen of Morlandria. Take them away!"

Arnon stumbled when the guards roughly seized him. As they dragged him through the doorway, his parents after him, he could hear Zaria's mocking voice.

"Now we shall see who will rule this planet, and we shall see about this Christianity that has deceived these poor fools!"

Olga Von Kemp had never been so miserable. Her face and hands were covered with scratches from the vines and briars of the jungle. She felt she had wandered for hours. Her tongue was swollen with thirst, and more than once she had heard the screams of jungle beasts. She had cowered in trees then, and, only because she knew she would die if she did not find her way back to Memphis, did she force herself out of them.

Time had lost its meaning, so she was somewhat shocked to see the outline of the city as she scrambled up over a wooded ridge. She stood a moment, gasping and thinking, *It won't do any good to go back to our ship. They'll be waiting there for me. I'll have to get help somewhere else.* As she stumbled toward the city, the only source of help she could think of was the Space Rangers.

At first she muttered to herself, "No, they hate me. I couldn't go to them."

However, there seemed to be no other choice. She staggered into Memphis and began roaming the streets, hoping to see one of them. *I know they're here somewhere,* she thought. *They've come for rest and relaxation. They've got to be here!*

And then she caught sight of Jerusha Ericson coming out of a shop with a package in her hand. "Jerusha!" Olga cried and reeled forward.

Jerusha looked at her with astonishment. "Olga, what's the matter?"

In brief, jumbled fashion, Olga blurted out her story. Then she begged, "You have to help us! They're going to kill Karl! I just know they will!"

"You come with me, Olga. We've got to get to the *Daystar!*"

Once aboard the cruiser, Jerusha took Olga directly to Captain Edge's cabin. There both she and the captain stared at the battered girl and listened as she told what had happened.

"They're going to kill him! I know they will."

"I'm afraid she may be right, Captain," Jerusha said. "There's something very bad going on."

"And I think *you're* right." Captain Edge sat thinking. Then he nodded shortly and said, "This is what we're going to do . . ."

11

Discovery at the Shrine

Lights set in the side walls gave off an eerie pale green glow as Mei-Lani, Bronwen, and Zeno wandered farther and farther down a corridor leading deeper into the earth. Who would put lighting in an abandoned shrine?

Mei-Lani stopped their progress from time to time so that she could study the writings and drawings on the walls. She noticed that, whereas the carvings on the upper level had talked about the "God of Heaven," those on the lower walls were talking about something far different.

Bronwen appeared very nervous, for she did not like the underground.

Thrax, however, had lived most of his life in a cave on his native planet, where everyone lived in caves. One time he took Bronwen's arm and murmured, "Don't worry. You'll get used to it."

"What do you make of all these drawings, Mei-Lani?" Bronwen asked.

Mei-Lani squinted, studying the detailed etchings that covered this section of the wall. "Bronwen, these tell the story of a mighty war in the heavens. A great angel decided that he would try to overthrow the Lord God of Hosts. It's just like the biblical account of Lucifer. This great angel deceived a third of God's angels with his beauty and power, and they mounted an attack against God." She pointed to another set of drawings. "Here, God sent another great angel to fight for Him. He's a lot more powerful than the first great angel."

They moved on to the next drawings. "Here, the first angel was defeated and thrown out of the heavens." Mei-Lani pointed to several more places on the wall. "But see, Bronwen—all the *names* have been scratched off except on this one drawing."

It was the picture of a beautiful woman standing at a window. Below the window stood many people, and in their midst was an altar. There was an inscription that read:

> I am Astarte, Queen of Heaven.
> Without the shedding of blood
> there is no remission of your sin.
> Make sacrifices to me
> and I will give you your heart's desire.

Bronwen said, "I've never seen anything more hideous—or more blasphemous!"

She had no sooner finished speaking than Thrax said, "Hold it just a minute. There's something up ahead." He stepped in front of the two women and drew his Neuromag. "Let me go first."

Stealthily Zeno started to move, his pale eyes searching the dim passage ahead.

Mei-Lani knew Thrax could see better than either she or Bronwen could, for his eyes were adjusted to living in faint light.

"There's something up there," he said. "You two wait here."

"No, we'll all go together," Bronwen said.

Mei-Lani and Bronwen both drew their weapons and followed the first officer forward until they came to a T in the corridor. A steel door was set in the wall straight ahead, and corridors led off right and left.

Thrax edged the door open and peered inside. Then he pushed it open wider and said, "Look at this, ladies."

Mei-Lani had to stand on tiptoe to see past him. She said, "It's so dark I can hardly see anything." Then she saw a figure. "Why, it's *Karl!*"

"Karl? Karl Bentlow?" Bronwen asked. She crowded forward. "It is! What's he doing here?"

"I don't know, but he's not here of his own free will. That's for sure," Mei-Lani said. "Karl! Karl!"

"Not so loud," Thrax said. "We're not sure who's around. There must be guards. I'm going to take a look. You have your Neuromags on kill?"

"No, on stun," Bronwen said.

Thrax shook his head. "This is not the time for that."

"It's not the time to kill either. You go on, Zeno. We'll be all right," Bronwen said.

They watched him disappear around the corner, his Neuromag held in a ready position.

Zeno Thrax moved slowly and heard nothing. Then he came to a large cavern that had several small tunnels leading from it. Stalactites of different sizes hung from the ceiling.

This is about as hot and dry a cavern as I've ever been in, he thought.

Around the edges of the cave, a red glow emanated from gaps in the floor. He peered down into one and could see a river of molten lava flowing past about a thousand feet down. It was like a giant furnace down there. The smell of sulfur nauseated him.

And then he smelled something else. It was

methane gas. Humans born on Earth could not distinguish the odor of methane, but Zeno from Mentor Seven could, and the smell was getting stronger. It was then that he bumped into a stalagmite. It crumbled to dust.

This place must get really hot to do this to a stalagmite!

At the center of the cavern Zeno saw a large stone altar. The top of the altar was a flat rock and had red dust all over it. Suspicious, the first officer took his datacorder from his belt.

This is human blood that has been reduced to dust by intense heat.

Bearing up the large flat altar rock were statues of gargoyles. Their grotesque forms were ominous signs of evil even for Zeno Thrax.

"Karl—Karl, can you hear me?"

Karl Bentlow was just coming out of a state of semiconsciousness. He thought he heard his name. He lifted his head, could see two shadowy figures standing outside his barred door, and all his fear came rushing back. "Who is it?" he whispered hoarsely.

"It's me—Mei-Lani—and Bronwen Llewellen. What are you doing here, Karl?"

Karl scrambled to his feet. Grasping the bars, he said, "It's that woman!"

"You mean Zaria?" Mei-Lani asked at once.

"Yes. Yes. The high priestess. She's the one that put us here."

"Where's Olga?"

"She got away or is being held someplace else. Or she's dead. I don't know. Get me out of here!"

"We don't have a key."

"You've got weapons, haven't you?"

"I don't think they'll touch anything here, but we'll

get word to Captain Edge. Right away. He'll do something."

Bronwen said, "I don't know if our communicators will work this deep underground, but we'll try." Touching the small box on her belt, she said, "Bronwen Llewellen to Captain Edge, condition red! Condition red!"

The box on her belt crackled with static, and then Edge's voice came in. "Edge here. Where *are* you, Bronwen?"

"We're underneath a shrine in the jungle—that shrine Mei-Lani told us about. We found *Karl Bentlow* here. He says that Zaria put him put here and is going to offer him for a sacrifice."

"All right. Hang on. Who's with you?"

"Mei-Lani and Commander Thrax."

"Don't let them take you. We'll be there as soon as we can."

"Thank you, Captain."

Thrax came hurrying back just as Edge's message ended. "I hope he gets here soon," he said. "I've got a feeling things are going to get hot around here before too long. Really hot."

In the dungeon beneath the palace, Prince Arnon wept bitterly. He was sitting on the cold stone floor, holding his hands over his eyes. "What a fool I've been! What a fool!" he moaned.

He felt a touch then and looked up to see his parents. They sat down beside him. Their arms went about him, and his father said, "We all make mistakes, my son."

Queen Teman kissed her son on the cheek and said, "We're going to have to trust God to get us out of this if He so wishes."

Always before when she had mentioned God, Arnon had sneered. But not this time.

"Let me tell you about what a God we have."

He lifted his tearstained face, and his mother began speaking. She related several stories of how God had delivered His servants—from a lions' den, from a violent storm, from a prison . . . Her eyes were warm as she said, "Our situation is no different."

"But, Mother, that was a long time ago."

"Time doesn't mean anything to God," Queen Teman said. "He's timeless. He always was, and He always will be."

"Yes, *people* are bound by time," the king said. "We think our few years are long. But with God a day is as a thousand years, and a thousand years is as a day."

Hope began to glow in Arnon, and he grasped his parents' hands, asking almost desperately, "Do you really think Jesus can deliver us?"

"If He so pleases. He can do all things. He made the universe, didn't He? He made the very bodies we have. He can save those bodies and set us free. Can you believe that, my son?"

They had nothing but time, and for the next few hours two loving parents once again delivered the gospel of Jesus Christ to their son. They spoke of His death on the cross and of how God said, "Turn to Me and be saved, all the ends of the earth."

"It's the blood of Jesus that saves, and all you have to do to have all your sins forgiven is simply to confess that you have sinned and ask Him to save you."

"Is that all?" Arnon asked. He again thought of his past and what a fool he had been. He whispered, "If Jesus can forgive me, I will have Him as my God."

As their son bowed his head, the parents began to pray. Soon they were rejoicing, for Prince Arnon had found the One who was many times greater than the powers that had bewitched him.

12

The Rescue

Captain Edge looked at the faces gathered about the conference room table. His own face was grim. "We just got a message from Mei-Lani. She's trapped under that shrine she told us about." He briefly told what he knew.

"Then we've got to save her!" Ringo cried. "Let's go!"

"Wait! Wait a minute! We don't know what we're getting into there, and we can't leave the ship. We've got another emergency."

"What's that, Captain?" Raina asked.

"It's the royal family. The high priestess has struck. We've just gotten word from one of the loyal members of the household that Zaria has imprisoned king, queen, and prince in the castle dungeon. It's well guarded, so we're going to have to fight our way to them, I think."

Dai Bando had been silent, just studying his captain's face. Now he asked, "Sir, how can we be in two places at once?"

"We can't. We'll just have to move very fast."

"Which shall we do first, Captain?" Dai asked. "I'm very worried about my aunt." His concern was revealed in his eyes.

"I think we'll have to go to the shrine first, Dai, but there's no time to lose. Here's what we'll do. We'll take the *Daystar* and hover over the shrine. We'll descend on ropes and attack as quickly as we can. Unfortunately, we don't know what sort of force we'll be meeting, and there aren't many of us."

"We can do it," Ringo said with excitement.

"Can I take Contessa, Captain?"

Suddenly Edge grinned. "Maybe you should. If she gives Zaria and her followers as much trouble as she's given me, I'll give her a big kiss."

Jerusha smiled. "I'll hold you to that, Captain."

"All right. Full armament. Lieutenant Jaleel, you'll see to the immediate arming of the party."

"Yes sir!"

"You'll have to stay aboard, Jerusha."

"No sir!" Jerusha cried. "I'm going with the party!"

"You'll do as I say! I'll be gone, and the first officer's gone. You'll stay on the bridge. And if anything goes wrong, no rescue parties. Understood?"

Jerusha stared at the tall captain. "But, sir—"

"Jerusha, this is no time for sentiment! We have to go, and someone has to stay. Now I want your word that, if we get into trouble, you won't come crashing in and be a casualty yourself." He put a hand on her shoulder and smiled. "You've become pretty special to me."

Jerusha swallowed hard. "Please be careful, Captain!"

"They can't kill me. I was born to hang," he said cheerfully. Then he turned to Lieutenant Jaleel. "Are we ready, Lieutenant?"

"All armed, Captain." She was carrying a new weapon, a Positron Turbomag. It operated on the same principle as the Neuromag but was many times more powerful. It was designed as an assault weapon.

Jaleel's eyes swept over the others, who were similarly armed. Holding up the Turbomag, she said, "These things would stop anything, Captain. They would even stop a Nagoid bull cresour," she said, naming the most fierce creature in the galaxy, a monstrous beast reportedly the size of five elephants.

"All right. Here we go. Here's where your training comes in, Lieutenant Jaleel."

Ringo had been outspoken about going, but now, standing next to Raina and ready to descend from the *Daystar* into the jungle, he said, "I don't mind telling you, Raina. I'm scared green. I don't even know if I can get down those ropes or not."

Raina patted his arm. "You'll do fine. I know you will, Ringo. We've got to do it for our crew."

The descent involved wrapping a silken rope around one leg to take the strain, then holding onto the Turbomag with one hand and the rope with the other. As Ringo stood at the open port, he grew slightly nauseated as he looked down at the top of the trees and the white shrine.

As the ship hovered in place, steady as a rock, Tara Jaleel snapped, "All right—go!"

Ringo threw himself out, aware that the others were right beside him. The rope bit into the upper part of his leg, and his hand grew warm as he slid downward. He dared not look down, and it came as a shock when his feet struck the earth. He collapsed and rolled over but came up at once to see that all the others were safely down as well.

The lines immediately began to be retracted, as Tara Jaleel, battle light in her dark eyes, commanded, "Come on, and don't spare anyone! These are our companions and our fellow warriors!"

Ringo raced beside Heck and Raina, but Dai Bando stayed step by step with Tara Jaleel.

The weapons officer looked to be running as fast as she could toward the arched entrance to the shrine.

Ringo thought she probably was feeling some irritation, knowing that Dai could easily have pulled away from her. "Don't get ahead of me!" she ordered.

"All right, Lieutenant!"

At that moment, even as Ringo was looking at Dai and Jaleel, there was a crackling, and something exploded between the two of them, blowing both off their feet.

"Take cover!" Jaleel yelled. "We'll have to fight our way in!"

Dai Bando knew Tara Jaleel was an expert in the art of warfare of all kinds, but they surely had the worst of all situations. The enemy was inside, well entrenched, and had weapons that could kill instantly. It was a miracle that she and Dai had survived the opening volley.

"We've got to get through that entrance, Dai," she said. "And they can see us coming." She fired her Turbomag and then shook her head in frustration. "They've positioned their sharpshooters by the door. It's like putting thread through a needle. It's suicide for anyone to get close to it!"

"Do you think if we got past them we'd be all right?"

"I think so, but I don't see any way to do it. You couldn't take five steps without one of those marksmen in there picking you off."

Dai said nothing, but he suddenly put down his Turbomag and stood up.

"*What are you doing?* They'll kill you! Get down, Dai!" Lieutenant Jaleel shouted.

But Dai Bando was running. He did not, however, run directly at the arched entrance where the enemy lay. Instead, he raced at right angles to it, then turned more quickly than anyone would have believed possible and ran in the opposite direction.

An explosion crackled at the spot where he had been—but Dai was gone. Once again, he turned and ran the opposite way. The gunfire continued, but always it was directed to where he had been, not where he was.

"He'll never make it!" Raina cried out. "We've got to do something, Jaleel!"

"Train your fire on that doorway! We'll give him cover fire as best we can!" But she knew it was hopeless. No human being could sprint a hundred-yard stretch of bare ground with marksmen firing constantly.

Nevertheless, Jaleel opened fire, and the others did as well. She also somehow managed to watch Dai Bando at the same time.

He was like a rocket, a rocket that could change direction. Once he leaped straight up, seconds before the ground beneath him exploded. As he dropped back to the earth, his legs were already churning. Now he was within fifty feet of the entrance . . . twenty-five feet . . .

"They can't miss now! He's too close!"

Then Dai Bando, from twenty feet away, launched himself into the air. Lieutenant Jaleel saw underneath his feet the streaks of fire from enemy weapons, while Dai hurtled through the air in one tremendous leap. Suddenly he had disappeared into the dark opening, and the gunfire ceased.

"He made it!" Jaleel said. She assumed that Dai, once inside, would be able to disarm the soldiers. Still, as she ran, she knew she was risking her life, gambling on the young Ranger's strength and speed and fighting ability.

The rest of the rescue party was behind her—she

heard their pounding feet. Then she was at the entrance. When Jaleel stepped inside, the first thing she saw was five enemy soldiers lying on the floor. They were dressed in black with the sign of Astarte emblazoned on their chests. Three of them were stirring slightly, but their faces were battered. The other two lay completely still.

"You did it!" Raina cried. She ran to Dai and threw her arms around him. "I was sure you'd be killed!"

Dai blushed and patted her back awkwardly. "Why, it wasn't all that hard."

"We don't have time for delays," Jaleel said. "We've got to get to that dungeon—wherever it is."

The rescue itself did not take long. Most of the guards surrendered at once when they saw the overwhelming force that they had not expected.

Finally, Edge and Thrax could greet each other.

"So this time you got into a hole you couldn't get out of."

"That's right, Captain. And we're very glad to see you."

"We've got to find Duke Zeigler—fast, Zeno. He's the only one that can help us get into the palace."

"What do we want to get into the palace for?"

"That's right—you don't know. Well, Zaria has taken over the kingdom. She's put the king, the queen, and the prince into the dungeon, and we've got to get them out. I was ordered not to tell you before, but that's why we came to this planet." He quickly revealed the essence of their secret mission.

Thrax said, "All right, Captain. We'll have to move quickly, indeed. That woman, from what I've heard, isn't likely to spare them long."

"Let's go!" Captain Edge yelled. "Back to the *Daystar!*"

13

Furry Hero

Y ou gonna tackle *Zaria?*"

Duke Zeigler stared at Mark Edge in disbelief. His light hair was falling in his eyes as usual, and his tall, lanky body was bent over almost in the shape of a question mark as he added, "Man, you got to be out of your mind!"

"What's the matter with you, Duke?" Edge asked, his eyes narrowing. "I've seen the time when you would fight a bear and give it the first bite!"

"Yeah. A bear is one thing, but this babe is something else. Let me tell you a little bit about her."

Zeigler twisted himself as if loosening his bones, and a thoughtful look came into his pale blue eyes. "I don't believe in kiss and tell, but a long time ago me and Zaria had quite a thing going."

"You mean you were romancing the *high priestess of Astarte?*"

"Naw, man, she wasn't that then! She was seventeen years old. But I can tell you, even then she was something else."

"What do you mean, 'something else'?"

"I mean she had a way of makin' things happen that I didn't quite understand. I didn't dig it, you know?"

"What kind of things, Duke?"

"Well, it's hard to explain. She was into some kind of religion even then. And when she'd get a certain look in her eye, I'd feel real funny down on the inside, you know?"

"No, I don't know—and I don't think I want to!"

"Well, I'll tell you what I found out about her. I don't like to admit it, but she shook me up. I'm not afraid to tackle any man head-on, but she was messin' with my mind, and I decided to split." Zeigler paused and scowled at some memory.

"So what happened then?"

"Well, she didn't say much when I told her. But after that, funny things started to happen. In the first place I nearly lost my mind. I don't know what she done, but I'd have these awful, terrible nightmares. Besides that, two times I nearly got potted."

"You mean somebody took a shot at you?"

"That's what I mean."

"Well, you have lots of enemies, Duke . . ."

"I didn't have that many back then." He tried to grin, but the troubled expression stayed on his face. "And I figured Zaria had put out a contract of some kind on me."

"So you're saying she's one bad tomato?"

"She's one bad tomato!"

"Can't help that. We've got to get the royal family out of that dungeon."

"Well, I can raise up kind of a small army . . . but we don't know what we'll meet up with when we get in there."

"I'll tell you what we want to do, Duke. I need for you to mount an attack on Zaria's temple."

"Are you crazy, Mark? That temple is one of the most guarded buildings in the city. Zaria's soldiers are fanatics. They would throw themselves off a cliff if she ordered them to."

"I know that. But if you attack the temple, most of her soldiers will leave the palace to defend the *temple*. The temple is their holy place. Nothing is more sacred to them except the high priestess herself. They'll rush to the temple in a heartbeat! After all, the royal family is secured in the dungeon, and King Denethor's followers won't counterattack for fear of Zaria finishing them off. That's what they'll think."

"How can my ragtag army hope to beat Zaria's soldiers?" Duke complained. "You're asking me to sign a death warrant on my friends!"

"Duke, all you have to do is attract attention. Stage several attacks, then draw back. Stage several more attacks, then draw back. We don't need for you to *win*. I just need enough time for my crew to get down to the dungeon and free the king. We can take care of Zaria and her soldiers after the royal family is safe."

"Well, OK," Duke said doubtfully. "Maybe it'll work." Again, he tried to grin. "If they kill us, they can't kill us but once, can they?"

"That's my old buddy! But if we play it smart, they won't kill us at all. Let's get going."

"Well, it looks like we've got the whole crew here," Jerusha said to Captain Edge.

"Maybe I should have left more to mind the store, but we don't know what we're going to meet in the palace once we get inside."

"The big question is," Jerusha said, "once we get in, can we get back?"

Edge smiled briefly at the girl. "You're pretty sharp, Jerusha. I figure this is going to be a tough attack. I think you'd better stay at the back and let the menfolks spearhead this."

"I didn't read anything in my contract about staying in the back! *You* go stay in the back!"

At this Contessa whined and attempted to get at her favorite captain. Jerusha held onto her short leash and scolded the dog. "Contessa, be still! I don't know why you're so crazy about this man anyway! He never shows you any attention!"

"It's my fatal charm. All dogs and women love me."

"You're the most egocentric person I ever met!"

"Yeah, I think a lot of myself, too." Edge winked at her, then grew dead serious. "All right. Everybody set?"

He let Tara Jaleel, second in command on this raiding party, check the crew. As Edge had said, every man and woman aboard the *Daystar* was there.

Studs Cagney lifted his Neuromag. "Yeah, let's go get 'em, Cap!"

"Everybody set your Neuromag on kill," Tara Jaleel said, "but it may come down to hand-to-hand fighting. Be ready." She glanced at Heck, who was struggling to adjust his weapon. "Now is when you will wish you had spent more time studying Jai-Kando."

"Not me," Heck said. He was wearing a specially designed uniform, which was somehow purple, green, and orange. "Just watch my smoke, Lieutenant!"

"You think you're going to blind them with that outfit?" she demanded. "Well, never mind. We're going in!"

As they followed the captain, Jaleel said, "I hope that bribe I paid will get us in through the secret entrance."

First Officer Zeno Thrax was walking beside her. "The trouble is, anybody that you can bribe can be bribed by somebody else."

"Maybe so, but I put a pretty good scare into him, too. He said the door would be unlocked, and he gave me the times when the guards are changed. We should be able to go right through and get to the lower part of the castle where the dungeons are."

Captain Edge, holding his Positron Turbomag at

ready, stepped through the outer door and swung the weapon around. "Nobody here!" he announced. "Come on! And be as quiet as you can. No sense attracting any more attention than we have to."

They took a set of stone stairs downward and soon found themselves in a dank lower corridor.

"This must be the way. It even feels like a dungeon, Captain," Jaleel said.

They wound along a labyrinthine passageway then, a cave corridor, twisting and turning past occasional stalagmites and stalactites until abruptly arriving at a dead end. A huge steel door barred their way.

"I wonder why there are no guards posted?" Tara puzzled. "Probably because nobody could get through that door. Look at the size of it! And no place for a key that I can see."

"See that up there?" Mei-Lani, standing directly in front of the steel door, was pointing upward to a strange symbol. "That may be the lock. An electronically operated code of some kind."

Captain Edge frowned in thought. "So how do we get access?" he murmured, mostly to himself.

No one had the answer to that, and all stood uncertainly, highly aware that guards might come pouring in at any moment and that they were trapped.

It was at that exact moment that Contessa chose to show her affection for Captain Edge. She made a tremendous leap onto his back.

Edge pitched forward. "Hey—" he yelled and went careening into a stalagmite.

They had come upon many stalagmites in the passage, but this stalagmite moved! He was certain it had moved!

"Contessa," he said, "get *off* me! Something's going on here."

"Come away, Contessa!" Jerusha tapped the huge dog on the nose. "What is it, Captain?"

"The door!" Raina shouted. "It's opening!"

Springing to his feet, Edge grinned. "Pushing that stalagmite must be the way the door is opened. No one would ever guess that, since stalagmites are so common in here."

"Well, you'll have to thank Contessa," Jerusha said.

"Yes, I guess I will, but later." He went through the door and found the royal family standing and staring at him.

"Thank God," the king said. "We thought it would be the torturer coming—or the executioner."

"Not so, Your Majesty. We've got to fight our way out of here, but I think everything's going to be all right."

Tara Jaleel said, "There must be hundreds of guards. Some of them are bound to intercept us on our way out."

"I can't even *remember* the way out!" Captain Edge said. "We made so many turns."

But the king said, "Not all of my servants have deserted us. If I can get to the key ones, we will have a small army of our own. Let us start—and pray that God will be with us."

The king himself led the way back up the stairs. He puzzled over the fact that they were encountering only a handful of Zaria's soldiers.

"This is certainly peculiar," Denethor said under his breath as he paused and listened. "The palace should be crawling with temple guards. I wonder where they all are?"

"King Denethor, forgive me for not telling you,"

Captain Edge said. "But there hasn't been enough time. I asked a friend of mine to attack the temple."

"*Attack the temple!* That's foolhardy. It's better protected than even the palace." Denethor's brow creased. "Who is this friend?"

"His name is Duke Zeigler."

"Duke Zeigler! How could you put our lives in *his* hands? He has a foul reputation on Morlandria!" the king said sternly. "He's the very kind that would betray us to Zaria. I've even heard he is in love with her. He'd obey her slightest command!"

"No, that was then, and now is now. Duke is an old friend of mine, Your Highness. He has his problems, but he has never broken his word to me. Zaria has lost her grip on him. I'm sure of it!"

At that moment, Prince Arnon interrupted. "Father, I think I know where Zaria is. If we can capture her, we can control her temple soldiers."

"Where is she?"

"She will be at the Shrine of Ugarit, offering sacrifices to Astarte. She says her high priestess powers come from there."

"Captain Edge," the king murmured, "there is an old tunnel leading from the palace to an altar located directly below the shrine. It is the Altar of Astarte, and it is in a huge cavern where my ancestors for millenniums sacrificed human blood. The place shames us, but—"

"Lead the way!" Edge exclaimed.

As the king led the *Daystar* crew through the musty connecting tunnel, Heck could scarcely see two feet in front of him. "Spiders and bats . . . spiders and bats . . . I've got to get out of here!"

Jaleel stepped back beside him. "What's wrong with you, Ensign? What are you muttering about?"

All Heck could say was "Spiders and bats . . . spiders and bats . . ." over and over again.

"So you're afraid of spiders and bats, huh?" Jaleel shook him like a rag doll. Then she pulled Heck's face close to hers and threatened, "If you don't shut up, spiders and bats are nothing compared to what I'll do to you!" The Masai warrior released him, saying, "If I hear another peep out of you, you'll regret it."

Heck nodded slowly and whispered so softly that only he himself could hear, "Jaleel, spiders, and bats . . . Jaleel, spiders, and bats . . ." Yet somehow he found the courage to put one foot in front of the other as they proceeded through the tunnel.

As Bronwen, Jerusha, and Raina brought up the rear, Bronwen voiced her concern to the girls. "King Denethor and our captain and Jaleel all think they have a chance to beat Zaria with Turbomags. I fear they are in for a rude awakening. Zaria, the poor girl, is just an instrument of the kingdom of darkness—our fight is not with her! It is with the fallen angels! Satan doesn't fear any weapon that men can make."

"Bronwen," Jerusha asked, "what are we going to do, then?"

"You and Raina wait for a signal from me. When you see it, come up behind me and pray. The powers of darkness are very strong here—as strong as I've ever felt! Indeed, be praying now."

Silently, King Denethor and Captain Edge led the rescue party out of the tunnel into the expanse of a large cavern. Edge gestured for continued silence, for there was Zaria, moving about the altar, her back to them, apparently preparing the sacrificial fire. Occasionally she looked up at a statue of Astarte and chanted mysterious words.

Mei-Lani exclaimed softly, "She looks so much like that woman we saw pictured—the woman in the window!"

Thrax looked at the idol and whispered to Edge, "That statue wasn't in here before, Captain. I wonder how they got a thing of that size into the cave."

King Denathor overheard his whisper. "The idol is kept behind a wall"—he pointed to the far side of the cavern—"until the time for human sacrifice. Then it is brought out."

As Edge's people cautiously approached the woman at the altar, Zaria suddenly turned to them and laughed loudly. "Did you think your little ruse to fool my soldiers would work, Captain Edge? I think not!"

The high priestess held up an arm and snapped her fingers. Instantly temple soldiers rushed into the cavern from the surrounding tunnels and surrounded Edge's rescue party, pushing them forward to the front of the altar itself.

"You meant for me to be the prey, Captain Edge, but I ensnared you in your own net."

Then Edge was stunned to see temple soldiers bring Duke and his men into the cave in chains. They had been beaten badly.

Suddenly Tara Jaleel shouted, "Defensive Perimeter Alpha Tango—*now!*"

Captain Edge, the *Daystar* Rangers, and Zeno Thrax encircled the royal family, their Turbomags held at the ready, while the captain frantically groped for some way to get them all out of this mess without getting everyone killed. He was not coming up with any ideas. They were surrounded, and the only way out was to use the Turbomags, which he was reluctant to do.

"Captain . . ." Zeno Thrax's whisper sounded urgent.

"What is it, Zeno?"

"Captain, we *can't* use the Turbomags. We'd all be blown to bits!"

"What are you talking about?"

"There's methane gas in the cave. I can smell it."

"Methane is odorless."

"It's odorless to you humans from Earth, but on my planet our sense of smell is different," Thrax continued. "Captain, if we fire the Turbomags, the super-hot blasts will ignite the methane. We will surely all die."

"Then why doesn't the fire by the statue ignite the methane?"

"I don't know—I haven't figured that out yet." Thrax looked around the cavern. "There must be a coal mine somewhere around here. The gas is seeping out of the walls, I think. And most of it is falling through the vents to the lava flow below us. That's my best guess, anyway. And why that doesn't ignite, I don't understand, either."

Edge didn't take long to come to his decision. "Everyone drop your weapons!"

Jaleel hissed loudly, but presumably even she could see the sense of it. It was better to fight hand to hand than die in a blazing inferno.

Edge's people dropped their weapons to the cave floor.

"What is Jesus going to do now, my cousin?" Zaria mocked King Denethor. "Maybe after I sacrifice you to Astarte, you can ask Him yourself." She motioned to the guards to bring Prince Arnon forward. "Ah, my prince! You young fool! I want your father to witness your death."

124

"Zaria," Arnon said, "you deceived me once but not now. I know that Jesus is able to save us. But even if He doesn't, I have decided to worship Him alone."

Edge watched in despair as guards strapped the prince to the altar and a large knife was placed in Zaria's hand.

"Let's see how brave you are when this knife plunges into your heart and your blood flows freely to the ground," the high priestess said. "Then I will toss your lifeless body on the sacrificial fire. There is no Jesus that will save you now!"

Then, with amazement, Edge saw Bronwen Llewellen start toward the altar. Jerusha and Raina followed her, and the girls appeared to be praying. The captain took a step forward, but Dai Bando gripped his arms. The boy seemed to understand what his aunt was doing, though Edge certainly did not. Perhaps Dai thought his captain would just get in the way.

Then Bronwen spoke to Zaria, sternly but with compassion. "You believe that Astarte is a powerful goddess"—she nodded toward the statue—"but I am here to tell you that the being you worship is nothing more than a wicked spirit."

Zaria's malignant eyes turned to Bronwen. "Astarte is the Queen of Heaven. She is the most powerful of all gods."

"Zaria, my God is Jesus Christ. It is He who is King of kings and Lord of lords. He is the almighty God! The dark spirit behind Astarte is nothing more than a servant of Satan. Let all these go, or you'll suffer the consequences!"

"You gray-headed old hag, what can you do to me?" Zaria screamed.

"I agree with you. I myself can do nothing. But, as it is written, Christ can."

125

"And where is your Christ?" Zaria shouted.

"He is here, if you had eyes to see."

"Where?" the high priestess scoffed. "I am looking all over the cavern. I don't see Him."

"You can't see Him because the eyes of your understanding have been darkened."

"This is nonsense." Zaria turned to Prince Arnon on the altar and lifted the knife above her head. Laughing, the high priestess looked back over her shoulder. "Jesus has no power over me."

Zaria turned to plunge the knife into Arnon's heart. But then she began struggling, twisting, turning in her effort to make the knife thrust. It appeared she couldn't lower the blade, no matter how much she tried.

She turned to the statue. "O Astarte, show us your power. Prove to these Christians that you are more powerful than Jesus Christ."

"Zaria, Zaria," Bronwen said, "the Lord Jesus loves you, and He asks you to surrender to Him. He doesn't want to hurt you—He wants to save you."

"Why do I need saving?" Zaria looked up at the ceiling and began chanting. At once all the temple soldiers joined her, and the cavern filled with the sound.

The cave floor shook. Several stalactites fell. From one of the floor vents near the altar a red gas drifted upward.

But Bronwen calmly turned to Jerusha and Raina. "Keep on praying. Do not take your mind off Jesus. The Lord can defeat the powers of darkness."

Contessa, the specially bred German shepherd, was standing with the group stationed about the king and queen. Suddenly she began to growl. Then she began to creep forward, through the chanting soldiers and toward the statue. The guards seemed too engrossed to notice her.

The red cloud swirled through the cavern like a whirlwind.

Bronwen never wavered. "I am a servant of Jesus Christ, saved for God's kingdom by His blood!"

And then Contessa, who had by now worked her way to the rear of the statue, launched herself at the idol's back. The statue of the goddess catapulted forward and crashed to the cavern floor. Contessa leaped to safety at the last moment.

And the red cloud shot through the floor vents to the molten lava below.

Now that the evil influence was gone, the temple guards for the first time were left to make their own decisions. They decided to run.

Again the cavern floor shook violently. Zaria collapsed. Dai leaped over the altar and threw her across his shoulder. Then he headed for the palace tunnel.

Prince Arnon was still strapped to the altar stone, though the altar's supports had crumbled, dropping the stone to the floor. Denethor tried to get to the prince, but the fleeing temple soldiers swept him with them into one of the tunnels. He loudly and desperately called his son's name. "Arnon! Arnon! Somebody save my son!"

And then Contessa leaped into action again. As vents in the floor began opening up everywhere, the dog pulled Arnon's bindings away from the altar stone with her strong teeth and jaws. She dragged the prince into the palace tunnel just as there was an intense explosion and the cavern roof caved in, collapsing the Shrine of Ugarit forever.

14

The New Karl

I've always thought," Jerusha mused, "that Karl was just rotten!"

"*I've* always felt that underneath that arrogance there was a pretty nice fellow," Raina said.

"Well, it was buried awfully deep. You know what they used to say: beauty is skin deep, but ugly goes right to the bone."

"It's often hard for a person who has Karl's good looks and natural ability to keep his head. You know how it was at the Academy. He always made top grades, and the girls were always throwing themselves at him. Literally."

"Not me. I never liked him."

"Well, neither did I. But I truly think Karl has changed somehow. I think staring death in the face does that. We've done it a few times, haven't we? And you remember how . . . well . . . how *thoughtful* we became, I guess you might put it."

"And you think Karl has really changed? I doubt it!"

"Give him a chance, Jerusha. We all need a little maintenance work, and Karl needed a lot of it. But I've got hopes for him. I've been praying for him, and I think the Lord's going to work in him."

Jerusha kept this conversation in her heart. But as she watched Karl Bentlow, she discovered to her surprise that he was, indeed, different. His looks were still smashing, but his manner had changed. He spoke more quietly and, for the most part, managed to keep away from the boastful manner that had so offended her. The boy clearly had been considerably shaken by his narrow escape. Since his rescue by the crew of the *Daystar*, he had become very subdued—to the astonishment of Jerusha and everyone else.

Olga Von Kemp had been unnerved by her experience in the jungle. She had been absolutely certain that she was facing death, and for several days after the rescue she was withdrawn. However, Olga had a natural tendency to push unpleasant things out of her mind, and when Karl Bentlow continued to pay special attention to Jerusha Ericson, she began to grow aggressive.

One day Karl said, "I think it's about time for us to get the P54 ready for takeoff, Olga. Why don't you go start the countdown and check the ship out?"

"Why don't you do it yourself?" Her eyes grew hard and without waiting for him to reply, she snapped, "I know why! You're too busy chasing around after Jerusha Ericson, that's why! You look like a fool, Karl!"

Karl stared at her, speechless.

For some time Olga told Karl what a fool he was making of himself over Jerusha. "She doesn't care anything about you!" she yelled. "You know what she is— stubborn as a mule. And from what I hear, she's head over heels in love with the captain of their ship."

"That's silly!" Karl said. "He's much older than she is."

"You think she cares?" Olga challenged. "Just watch her the next time she's around him. She's like a puppy looking for someone to throw her a scrap. But Mark Edge has more sense than that."

Karl shifted his feet, finally saying, "To tell the truth, I've always been impressed with Jerusha. With her abilities, I mean."

Karl Bentlow went straight to the *Daystar* and reported to the bridge, where he found Captain Edge.

"I just wanted to thank you, Captain, for what you did."

"Well, I expect you need to thank Commander Thrax, Mei-Lani, and Bronwen, Bentlow."

"I've already done that, sir, but at least my thanks are to you for getting them there. And my congratulations on a successful mission. I'll be happy to pass this word along to the people in the Intergalactic command."

"Well, I need all the help I can get. My record's not any too good," Edge said.

"Do you think I could I see Jerusha, sir?"

"Sure. She's checking over the ship. She's a topflight engineer. Never saw a better one!"

Karl walked through the *Daystar*, speaking to several crew members on the way, and was pleased to find that they remembered him. He found Jerusha in the central engine core, adjusting the intermix modulator.

"I just came to say good-bye, Jerusha."

Jerusha straightened up. She was wearing her regular uniform and had a smudge of grease on her face. "I guess we'll be taking off soon, too," she said.

"You have some grease on your cheek. Mind if I take it off?" He pulled a spotless handkerchief from his pocket, reached out, and removed the grease. "There—" he smiled "—that looks better."

Jerusha kept her eyes on Bentlow as he talked about their preparations for leaving. After a time, she cocked her head to one side and murmured, "Karl, something's different about you. You're not the same as you used to be."

"I guess nearly getting killed can change a fellow's mind about things," he said ruefully. "I've been looking back over what I've done, and I'm not too proud of it." He swallowed hard. "There's something I want to tell you, Jerusha, but it's hard to say."

"Why, just say it."

The girl looked very attractive, which made Karl feel strangely awkward for him. He looked down at his feet and shifted his weight again. Then he spread his hands in a gesture of helplessness. "I've never liked to admit that anyone is better or smarter than I am. But even at the Academy I knew that you were, and it always made me feel . . . well . . . inferior."

"I never knew you felt like that! But there was no need."

"Well, I did. And all the crude remarks I've made were just a smoke screen to cover it up. So I guess this is where I say I'm sorry for all my rotten behavior."

Jerusha seemed moved by his apology. She put out her hand and said, "I believe in forgiving and forgetting, Karl. Let's put it all behind us and start all over again." And she smiled at him.

Relief washed through Karl. He took her hand and squeezed it hard. "That's fine of you, Jerusha. I don't know how you can forgive that quickly. When somebody crosses me, I just want to get even."

"It's because the Lord Jesus forgave me."

Then he realized that he was still holding the girl's hand, and he released it abruptly. Passing his hand over his hair, he said nervously, "Hearing anybody say that sort of thing always makes me uncomfortable."

"That's because Commander Inch brainwashed you. She made you think that Christianity was just a myth."

Karl thought and then nodded. "I guess that's right! She did. I don't know why she hates Christianity so much."

"Jesus demands everything from a person, Karl, and Commander Inch hasn't got to the point where she's ready to give up. All of us must come to that point. I know I did. I'm afraid I was a little bit proud of my abilities, and I didn't realize that there were some things I couldn't handle. Do you mind if I tell you about how I became a believer?"

"I—I guess not."

"Then sit down here. We've got a few minutes."

For the next fifteen minutes, Jerusha, in a simple way, spoke of how she had come to the end of her rope and how she had no one to turn to. She then told him she had asked Jesus for forgiveness and to come into her life.

"And He did come. How can I explain it? Jesus is always with me—I never wake up alone. Even in the darkest hours of my life, I haven't been by myself, and that's what keeps me going. He said, 'I will never leave you.' I believe that, and I know that one day I'll stand before Him, and I want to be able to say that I was obedient."

Karl remained still for a long time, and then he said, "I've always thought that if I had a great ship like the P54, I'd have everything. But when I thought I was about to die, I knew that the biggest, best ship in the world isn't everything." He stood up.

"Karl," Jerusha said, "I think you're on your way to something wonderful."

"Do you, Jerusha?" There was something plaintive in his voice.

She gave him a sudden smile. Once again she put out her hands, and he took both of them. "I think you're going to begin a new adventure very soon."

Karl Bentlow was stirred by her words. He had never had trouble finding a girlfriend, but something different was attracting him to this girl. Now, without really meaning to, he suddenly leaned forward and gave her a light peck on the cheek.

Astonishment came into Jerusha's eyes.

"I'm sorry, Jerusha, but somehow I just wanted to do that."

"Well, you'd better not do it again!" she said, blushing. But she smiled.

Karl looked at her for a moment, and then he returned her smile. "Will I see you when we get back to Earth?"

"I would think so, but don't make too much of that kiss, Karl."

"No, I won't do that. Good-bye, Jerusha."

For hours afterward, he thought about Jerusha Ericson. He realized that she had a quality that he had not previously sought in girls, and somehow he liked it.

"She's some girl," he murmured to himself, thinking over the talk he had with her. "But a fellow would have to be a Christian to have a chance, and that leaves me out."

Jerusha was not able to stop thinking about her meeting with Karl Bentlow. She told Raina what had happened and wound up the story by saying, "I don't know what to think about it. He's so different!"

Raina looked at her. "And you let him kiss you?"

"I couldn't help it. He did it so quickly."

Raina smiled slightly. "He's had lots of practice. You'd better be careful. He's putting the moves on you."

"Raina, I don't think he is. He's tried that ever since I've known him, but there was something different about Karl today. He wants to get together with me the next time we're on Earth."

134

"What about Olga?"

"I don't think she matters as much to Karl as she'd like to."

"Just be careful," Raina advised. "I know he's handsome and charming and all of that, but he's not a believer, Jerusha."

"No, and I'm not thinking of him like that. But I do think we ought to pray that he would be saved."

"We'll do that."

They prayed right then for the young man and even for Olga. That was somewhat more difficult.

Then Jerusha went back to work.

But when Captain Edge passed by, she took one look at him and turned away. *I'm all mixed up. Everybody thinks I've got a crush on the captain. That's what they call it. A crush. It sounds like something silly, and maybe it is.* As she made her way to her cabin, she thought, *I guess it's just a matter of growing up. Too bad we can't just leap over the years between twelve and eighteen. Everything in between is really a pain!*

15

Celebration

I laugh every time I think of Contessa's infatuation with Captain Edge," Temple Cole said.

Mei-Lani giggled. "So do I. He looked so funny that time she knocked him into the buffet table. Remember? And then she sat on his chest and licked his face."

"I think he actually loves that dog, but he's too macho to say so now. It wouldn't be manly."

They were sitting in Temple Cole's cabin, where the doctor had invited Mei-Lani for tea. Takeoff was tomorrow, and Dr. Cole had been hoping to talk with Mei-Lani before the space voyage began. Abruptly she said, "Mei-Lani, you're a very precious girl. I've become very fond of you."

"Why—thank you, Dr. Cole."

"I wish you'd consider me as a friend."

"I do consider you as a friend, Doctor."

"Then, friends tell each other things, don't they?"

"They do. Do you want to tell me something?"

"No." Dr. Cole smiled. She took Mei-Lani's hand and looked directly into her eyes. "I want you to tell *me* something. You've had something buried in your heart that you want to tell, but you're afraid to say it out loud. Everyone has noticed it."

"They—they have?"

"All the girls have anyway. Jerusha and Raina and Bronwen Llewellen have all spoken of it to me. They say you are troubled about something, and we all love you so much we hate to see that. Don't you think you could tell me?"

Mei-Lani's cheeks flushed, and the scarlet tinged her neck. She looked away, then back again. "All right. I will." She seemed to struggle, but at last she said, "It's my face."

"Your face. What's wrong with your face?"

"It's—well, I've got makeup on now. I've learned how to conceal it a little but—Dr. Cole, *I've got pimples!*"

Temple sat holding Mei-Lani's hand, astonished, and then she began to laugh. "You mean all this time you've had us worried sick about you, and all it is is a bad complexion?"

Mei-Lani jerked her hand away. "You may think it's nothing, but *you've* got a good complexion! So do the other girls!"

"Of course we do, but you've forgotten one thing."

"What's that?" Mei-Lani said, still clearly unhappy with the doctor's laughter.

"We're all older than you are. You see, you are just at the age when most girls go through physical change. It's part of becoming a woman. That's all. My dear, let me assure you that this is entirely temporary. As you get older, the problem will clear up. Besides, no matter what your complexion was, we would all love you anyway."

Tears came to Mei-Lani's eyes. "Do you mean it, Doctor? Will they go away?" she asked hopefully.

"Of course! I'm surprised that you haven't noticed that this is a common thing with girls—and with boys too. It's just that, at your age, appearance is so very important."

"Isn't it important to you?"

Temple Cole smiled. "Yes, I must confess that it is. And I'll soon be having problems, like wrinkles, that won't go away with time. But yours will. I promise."

Mei-Lani took a deep breath, and then she laughed. "I've been so worried. I wish I had told you a long time ago."

"Always come to me or to one of your friends when you have trouble like this. Most likely you'll find out that others have had it themselves or, perhaps, something even more serious."

Temple Cole put out her arms and hugged the girl. "So that's over with. Now we can think about getting under way tomorrow—and about all the good things that lie ahead."

The palace banquet hall was enormous. "Why, you could put ten football fields in here!" Heck exclaimed.

As usual, Heck overstated, but it *was* a magnificent dining area. The tables were covered with snow-white cloths, the utensils were gold and glittered under the heavy cut-glass chandeliers, waiters and waitresses moved about dressed in maroon and white uniforms. And the food! The Space Rangers had never seen such food.

"I could get used to this," Heck said, as he enjoyed another mouthful. He said something else, but no one could possibly have understood him.

"You're going to choke!" Ringo said irritably. "You've got rotten table manners!"

"It won't matter when I'm rich," Heck replied when he could speak again. "Nobody cares what rich people do."

Denethor was seated on a platform along with the queen and the prince. At that moment the king arose and held up his hand for silence.

Instantly, a hush fell over the banquet hall.

"My friends, beloved subjects, and guests"—

Denethor's voice carried well to every table—"we are here tonight to celebrate the friendship that has been forged with the Intergalactic Council. As you know, Captain Mark Edge and his gallant crew arrived just in time to save us from total disaster."

Applause went up, and King Denethor waited, smiling, until it died down. "Tomorrow our friends must leave us, but before they do, I wish to publicly express to them a word of personal gratitude. The crown prince has asked permission to speak also, a request I have granted."

Prince Arnon arose and came forward wearing the royal robe of the House of Denethor. He said, "It is a miracle of God that I am here tonight. I must confess to all of you, as I have to my father and mother, that I failed sadly and was led astray." Then his face lighted up. "But my parents have forgiven me, and God has forgiven me, and now I ask for your forgiveness. I only desire that I may serve you well all of my days."

An enormous roar went up then, and every person in the banquet room stood to his feet, calling out, "We forgive you! Long live Prince Arnon and the House of Denethor!"

Arnon bowed and then returned to his seat.

When quiet was finally restored, the king said, "I believe we must give special praise to the *Daystar* Space Rangers. I will ask them to stand as I call their names. Jerusha Ericson—Dai Bando—Mei-Lani Lao—Raina St. Clair—Hector Jordan—and Ringo Smith. Will you come forward?"

Puzzled and more than a little nervous, the Space Rangers approached the platform.

When they were standing before him, King Denethor suddenly drew his sword.

Heck cried, "Look out! He's going to kill us!"

"Be quiet!" Raina said in exasperation. "He's not going to do any such thing!"

"All of you will kneel," Denethor said.

The Rangers did so, and the king went down the line, touching each on the shoulder and saying, "I give you the blessing of the royal House of Denethor and grant you permission to call upon us for any need you may have."

As soon as the ceremony was over, Heck was beside himself. "I know what I'm going to ask for," he confided to Dai. "Ten million dollars!"

He would have approached the king at once, but Dai grabbed him and put a hand over his mouth.

"Take him out of here if he won't be still!" Jerusha said.

Dai said in Heck's ear, "If I let you go, will you be quiet?" Receiving a nod, he removed his hand, but he kept a firm grip on Heck's arm.

"Now I have one further announcement," the king said. "Perhaps it is the most important of all. My wife and my son—come and stand here with me."

As the royal family stood together, the king announced loudly, "As you know, the high priestess of Astarte is in prison, where she can do no further harm. All places of Astarte worship will be torn down immediately. There will be no more human sacrifices. As a family, the crown will worship the Lord Jesus Christ, and we encourage everyone in our kingdom to do likewise."

There were loud cries of agreement with this, and Temple Cole whispered to the captain, "I see that the king is going to be quite an evangelist. It will be interesting to see how it goes when the leader of the planet is a devout Christian."

"Now, Captain Mark Edge, will you please come

forward?"

"The king is calling for you," Temple said. "Go on!"

Mark obeyed, somewhat astonished, and the king looked at him fondly. "Captain Edge, words can never express my gratitude."

"Your Majesty, I only did my duty."

"Many men try to do their duty, but few can perform it as magnificently as you." He turned to the prince, who handed him a gold chain, heavy and thick, having a gold pendant set with diamonds and other precious stones. "Lean forward, Captain!"

And Denethor slipped the beautiful necklace over Mark Edge's head.

While the captain still stood on the platform, the king smiled and said, "We have one more necklace to award." He accepted a smaller necklace from the queen. "Contessa, this is for you!"

Jerusha let out a gasp but then quickly said, "Come, Contessa!" She led the giant German shepherd to the king's dais and said firmly, "Sit!"

The dog sat quietly, her eyes on the captain, as the king said, "We owe much of our success to you, and it is always a pleasure to award a beautiful lady. So, Lady Contessa, here is your award." And he placed the second necklace about Contessa's neck.

There were other awards, but Mark Edge did not pay close attention. He was so fascinated by his beautiful necklace that he could not keep from staring down at it.

Then the dog was nudging his knee, and absently he leaned down to pet her. It was the first time he had ever done so. As he did, the necklace about his neck swung low and became entangled with the one around Contessa's neck. When he straightened up, the two necklaces tightened like a noose.

"Contessa!"

Startled by the sudden pressure on her neck and startled by Edge's cry, Contessa bounded forward. Her bulky weight pulled Edge off the awards platform. Turning a perfect flip, he landed flat on his back.

"Jerusha," he yelled, "Get this animal off me! She's ruining my necklace!"

Moody Press, a ministry of the Moody Bible Institute,
is designed for education, evangelization, and edification.
If we may assist you in knowing more about Christ
and the Christian life, please write us without obligation:
Moody Press, c/o MLM, Chicago, Illinois 60610.